TJ's Ride

Book One in The TJ Series

J.R. Hamilton

Dead Key Publishing

A Dead Key Publishing Book
Published by Dead Key Publishing
Denver, CO 80237, USA

This is a work of fiction. Names, characters, places, and incidents either are the product of the author's imagination or are used fictitiously, and any resemblance to actual persons, living or dead, business establishments, events, or locales is entirely coincidental. The publisher does not have any control over and does not assume any responsibility for author or third-party websites or their content.

Publication History
TJ's Ride: Book One in the TJ Series, ebook edition, 2014
TJ's Ride: Book One in the TJ Series, paperback edition, 2016

978-0692678510
0692678514

Acknowledgements

A man can live his entire life and never do the very thing he has wanted to do for years. I'm not talking about sailing around the world or something outrageous. I'm talking about something as simple as putting words on paper. This story has been beating around in my head for years, but every time I started putting it on paper I stopped for some reason. My wife, Joyce, has been after me for years to write but I just never got around to it and, quite honestly, I never thought it would be interesting to anyone else.

However, she was the first person who considered my ramblings as being worthy of publication. I seriously appreciate her support. But we all know how biased family can be about such things. Then I met Cher Smith, a published author, who became a cherished, beloved friend. She prompted me to finish this story, so I did, and with her editing help, this is the story that came out.

Another person who was instrumental in this book was my mother. She died many years ago, but she always prompted me to enjoy my imagination, even explore it and to never give up on my dreams. My mother had a number of sayings. "You can do anything you set your mind to" was one of them. She would say things like that when she was trying to motivate me to succeed. She also had one, "I brought you into this world and I'll take you out," which she used after I was too old to spank and she wanted to make a different kind of point.

There are many other people from whom I drew energy and who supported me in ways I can never express or even thank properly. Without friends to love, the world would be a dreary place.

There is another group of people I want to recognize here: those young ladies and gentlemen who are serving and have served their country. Having spent twenty-two years in the Navy, I have had the privilege of working shoulder to shoulder with many of them. During Viet Nam I served with many in the Marine Corp, Army, Air Force and Navy (I didn't ignore the Coast Guard; I just never served with them). These men and women have set their everyday lives aside in order to serve their country, even when they may not have agreed with everything that was happening. They all deserve our respect and thanks.

There is a subgroup of the above that I have the greatest respect for, those who have returned home who have been in any way harmed by their service. Please note that a portion of any profits from this book will be donated to Wounded Warrior Project in thanks for the wonderful work they are doing with our American heroes.

To all who took time to read and comment on my manuscript, thank you. I appreciate what I hope was honest feedback, even though most were from family and friends.

Lastly, though this should have been first, I thank God for giving me the imagination to bring this story to life. He rode with me through the darkest days of my life, even when I didn't know it or deserve it.

Some people believe that writers include

themselves in their books. Well, that is something of the case here. TJ Hamlin exists only in my mind but a part of me would very much like to be TJ. TJ is that unusual combination of toughness, self-confidence and kindness that I wish was. His adventurous spirit is very much like mine but as I have grown older I can only do many of these things by way of writing.

This is the first of TJ's adventures. I have a few more stored up in my head that I want to get on paper. If you will hang on and ride out this TJ story, I hope you find yourself craving another. Then my writing won't be in vain.

CHAPTER ONE

Protagonist George Webber wrote, "You can't go back home to your family, back home to your childhood ... back home to a young man's dreams of glory and of fame ... back home to places in the country, back home to the old forms and systems of things which once seemed everlasting but which are changing all the time—back home to the escapes of Time and Memory." From these few lines Thomas Wolfe came up with the title for his book *You Can't Go Home Again*. Whether you subscribe to this line of thought or not, I found it to be very true.

I joined the Navy and left home in December 1964. After Navy boot camp I received orders for specialized training, then to the Brown Water Navy patrol in Viet Nam. After my tour there I was assigned to attack squadrons with various ships in the Western Pacific. Perhaps this would make an interesting story in itself, and maybe someday, but that isn't the story I want to tell right now. In truth, that was a million years ago and really has nothing to do with who I am now.

In 1968 I received orders from LeMoore, California, back to my hometown of Corpus Christi, Texas. This was no surprise as it was part of my agreement with the Navy for volunteering to spend fourteen months in Viet Nam and a tour with attack squadrons on a few different carriers. It's many sailors' dream to be assigned a station in or near their hometown, and I was no different. I had dreams of riding with my old friends, spending time fishing for shark on Bob Hall Pier, and partying at Padre Island. Had I known what was coming, I'm not so sure I wouldn't have asked for orders to hell before accepting orders to the Naval Air Station backyard.

On my return to my hometown I discovered the truth being told by Mr. Wolfe through Mr. Webber. At first glance I thought everyone else had changed, the fact of the matter was they were the same, I had changed. They were the same people I had left, doing the same old things; they still talked about the game-winning touchdown, the game-saving block. They had been born, raised and now lived in the same twenty-mile circle while I had been to war, visited numerous countries, lived in other states and seen both amazing and scary things. They harbored the same old prejudices I once did but now found appalling after working with so many people of different ethnic and even native backgrounds. No, you can't go home again, not because home has changed but quite the opposite.

I was living in the enlisted men's barracks, a place I hadn't slept in once since leaving Navy boot camp, and I wasn't overjoyed by it. Even though my rating allowed me a two-man room, I missed the privacy my own apartment afforded me. It was still better than sharing sleeping quarters with seventy-five other men. Living on a Navy ship is not the greatest of joys. You get to know people all too well.

I had been out late partying with a few old and a number of new friends, and had consumed more than a little Jack Black. I couldn't figure out what all the noise was until I got my eyes open and realized it was after nine in the morning; I was almost two hours late for work. I went to the door to find Bill Rose, the first class I worked for, and the shop chief standing there. The chief and I got along pretty well but Bill was on my ass all day long. As a second class I was doing work that someone of a much lower pay grade should have been doing. To make a long story short, Bill wrote me up and pushed the charge to go as far up the ladder as possible. The fact that I threatened to kick his ass may have had something to do with him pushing so hard. Before I knew what was happening, I was standing in front of the squadron skipper, scared to death I was going to get busted.

The skipper gave me a royal chewing out then sent everyone out of the room but him and another captain I didn't know.

"Petty Officer Hamlin," the skipper said. "This is Captain Joseph of JAG. He wants to talk to you, but first I need to tell you something. Nothing you discuss in this room is ever to be spoken of beyond these walls unless you are otherwise directed. If you choose not to help Captain Joseph, there will be no retribution. But if you do, you will be assisting the Navy with a grave issue and I will make these charges go away." Captain Joseph offered his hand, and I shook it before taking a seat near the skipper's desk.

"Petty Officer Hamlin…wait, can we get on a first name basis?" Captain Joseph asked. "What do your friends call you?"

"Just call me TJ, sir, if that is okay with you," I replied.

"Oh? Why TJ?" he asked.

"My name is Thomas Jefferson Hamlin, sir, ergo, TJ."

"Okay, TJ. Have you ever used drugs?" Captain Joseph asked.

"Of course not" was the answer he expected, and that's what I gave him.

He grinned at me and looked at the skipper, who immediately got up and left the room. "Let me tell you what we know here, TJ, and maybe we can skip all the bullshit." He opened a file in his lap. "You work at a bar a few nights a week for a man named Louis Hornbuckle; in this bar are two dancers, Leslie and Jessi. On four occasions in the last three months you made trips to Mexico and brought something back with you for them. I know that you've been working some long hours and suspect you have to be using something to keep awake. What did you get for the girls and yourself in Mexico—and no more BS or I terminate this discussion, and everything in this file is released to legal."

I thought for a moment. *These guys are slipping,* I thought. I made a trip down to Mexico almost every week picking up Dexedrine, a light speed some people used to keep their energy level up, while others used it for weight control. I had been selling it to the girls and a few other dancers in the area at a profit you would not believe.

I looked at the captain. He was not playing around. "I picked up some dex," I said finally, "sometimes to help me stay awake and sometimes as a favor for someone else."

"Good," he said. "Now, with that out of the way maybe we can get to the point. There has been a huge increase of drug use in the Navy. A few weeks ago we busted a sailor selling pot and crystal meth. He told us a little, but not enough to be of any great assistance. What he did tell us leads us to believe you can be of great assistance in our investigation."

"Look, I don't go in for the heavy stuff, not pot or anything else," I stammered.

"We are pretty certain that is true, but we have an unusual opportunity here. Corpus Christi is your home town, is it not?" he asked, and I knew he already knew the answer. "Not only that, but you were a member of the CC Riders motorcycle club and are, or were, good friends with a man referred to as Mad Dog. Am I right so far?" he asked as he looked up from the file.

"I haven't even been in touch with any of the guys since I got back in town," I told him. "I don't even ride where they hang out."

"We know that too, but we want that to change," he smiled.

"I don't know what you're talking about or where this conversation is going but I don't think I like it. It sounds like you want me to bust on some brothers, and I want nothing to do with it. If that is all, sir, may I be excused?" I asked.

"You may not be excused, and I guess I need to clear up a point here that your skipper got wrong. He said that you could walk away from this and nothing would happen. That is wrong…very wrong. We have enough information and substantial proof to take you to a court martial and charge you with, to start with, possession and distribution of controlled substances. On the positive side, this will make you a civilian; on the negative side finding a job on a less than honorable discharge will not be easy. Is my point getting across now? Am I making myself understood?" He pulled a cigarette from his shirt pocket and offered me one, which I took.

I was beaten. I knew it but I couldn't just let it

be. "You guys are trying to make sure you see me dead. We aren't talking about a bunch of kids on motorcycles," I said. "We're talking about people who will do whatever they need to in order to keep their business alive, and if that means putting me in a hole, they really don't care. Some of these people may have been my friends years ago but that doesn't buy much in their world now if they are running drugs." I took a deep drag from the cigarette. "You really aren't giving me any choice, are you?"

"No, we aren't. I will do whatever it takes to stop the flow of drugs to the military. I'm tired of seeing our young men in hospitals, kicked out of the Navy or on morgue slabs. If placing one person at risk stops this, then yes, I'm willing to risk it. If I could do it myself I would, but we both know that wouldn't sell. We will do everything we can to protect you, but we need you out there getting information for us. This is no less a war than Viet Nam, and if we don't stop it we will lose a lot more of our young men."

"Stop drugs? You must live in a wonderful world but I thought Fantasy Land was only in Disneyland. Drugs are a fact in your Navy and they always will be. You may slow the flow from one source but another will come along to replace it."

He didn't look surprised by this. "No, we may not stop drugs in the Navy but I refuse to give up. I will do whatever it takes to attack this problem at every level."

I acted like I was thinking, but I knew I had no choice. This guy was almost fanatical. "Well, it appears you are giving me no choice, so how am I going to help in your little war?"

He gave me a look that told me he didn't see it as a little war. "We have arranged a job for you at a bar where we know some of the people hang out from time to time—they need a bouncer and you need a job. When you are not at work or sleeping I want you on the CC Rider's tail finding out how, when and where they are getting their drugs, who is distributing them and who is providing them. As far as anyone knows, you are no longer in the Navy. You will have to find a place to live, preferably not too far from your old friends. When this is all over, you will be returned to duty, apologies made and you will be advanced to the next pay grade and rewarded for your service," he said as he leaned back in his chair.

"How long do I have to play this silly-assed game?" I asked.

"Until you provide us with enough solid information and evidence to shut down this operation and put some outlaws in jail," he replied.

"Can I at least tell my mother so she doesn't go ballistic?" I asked.

"No. For more reasons than I want to explain, that is a bad idea. If anyone outside the very limited number of people finds out anything, you'll be placing their lives in danger. Let's just say that the less anyone knows, the better it is for you and them."

I thought about what I was hearing, and I wasn't too crazy about much of it. I knew the club did have an element that was involved with drugs, but I never thought it was this big. I was beginning to think that maybe I didn't really want to be a part of this. "You know, I'm not so sure I want any part of this. In the first place you are asking me to be part of an investigation that could end up in court, which means I would have to testify, in which case my life expectancy is about –"

"Petty Officer Hamlin!" he interrupted. "I

understand your concern, and we will do everything we can to protect you. If need be, we will transfer you anywhere you want in order to keep you safe, but let me make this as clear as possible. My primary concern is for the Navy now and the future of the Navy. If I have to sacrifice one man for that cause I will."

I sat there dazed. "Thank you, sir. I appreciate your honesty, but I don't feel one damned bit better."

He leaned forward in his chair. "TJ, I don't want to see you hurt any more than I want to see any other sailor in trouble with drugs. I will do everything in my power to protect you, but I need your help. You are probably the only person on this base, perhaps the one person in the Navy who can help me, and I'll be damned if I am going to let this opportunity slip through my fingers."

I was stuck. I had no escape from this without screwing myself completely. "Okay, I'm on board, but I can't survive out there on my own."

He leaned back again, relaxing. "No, we aren't leaving you hanging. Your contact is a woman named Jean Marie. She knows who you are and will be in touch in the next couple of weeks. I don't doubt that this could take several months, even a year or more, but you will be helping the Navy and will be saving lives along the way. For the next few months no one from the Navy will be in touch with you. If anyone says they are from the Navy and wants to talk to you, don't trust them and get in touch with Jean Marie as soon as you safely can. Other than Jean Marie, don't trust anyone. You already know how dangerous this can be, so you have to do everything possible to minimize that danger. When you leave this office you are a civilian; you can't let anyone know any different."

"I want all this in writing, otherwise you guys can court martial me and bust me, kick me out, whatever you want," I told him.

He smiled. "You act like you don't trust me."

"Honestly…hell no, I don't trust you. Basically you have already lied to me, threatened me with Mast and told me if I don't do this you are going to get me kicked out of the Navy, and you think I should trust you? Captain, I have tried to do my job for the Navy and take care of my family at the same time and because I've done a few things that bend the law a bit you want me to risk my life without a safety net? No way in hell!"

He thought for a moment. "This is more than I can do. I can't put this in writing without speaking to someone about it."

I was angry now. "Fine, do whatever you want, talk to whoever, but I am off the radar until you get straight. I'm out of here." I headed for the door.

"TJ, I will talk to the people I need to. I will see you in an hour," he said.

"Do what you have to. I will be in the enlisted man's club as soon as I change clothes. Find me there," I said and went out the door.

After changing my clothes I got on my Harley and turned out the gate instead of going to the club. Once outside the gate, I headed for Padre Island Drive and twisted the throttle hard rolling the big bike past one-twenty. I knew if the cops stopped me at this speed I was jail bound, but at this point I really didn't care. I blew past two CC Riders—the distinctive rockers on the back of their cutoffs was easy to see. I grabbed the throttle and tube-locked it, leaving them in the dust.

When I started getting close to busier areas of Corpus Christi, I hit a median and flipped back toward the base. The two riders did a "U" turn and were soon on either side of me; one of them pointed at a bar up the road, and I pulled into the lot. One of the riders came over as I stepped off the bike.

"Hey, bro, you're TJ, right?"

I looked at the big man. "Yeah, but I don't think I know you," I said wearily.

"No, man, you don't know me, but you know Eddie, right?" he asked.

Eddie was one of the brothers I rode with years ago, before I joined the Navy. "Certainly I know Eddie. I haven't seen him in years."

"Eddie heard you were in town and told us to watch for you, said he saw you but couldn't get back to you and he told us what your bike looks like." He handed me a CC Riders card with Eddie's name on it. "He just wants to hear from you, bro. Give him a call." He returned to his bike, and the two men spun out of the parking lot.

I headed back to the base.

I went into the enlisted men's club and ordered a double single malt. This really felt like a drunk day, and I intended to end the pain of reality as quickly as possible. I was on my third double when a third class in sharp whites came in. "Captain wants to see you," he said almost as though he had power.

I finished my drink and followed him out, got on my bike and fired it up; the idiot in whites was standing there holding his vehicle's back door open. "I will drive you over," he said. I pulled up next to him and twisted the throttle, throwing dust all over his shiny white uniform, and headed for the captain's office.

When I walked into the office, the captain was waiting for me holding an envelope. I took it from him, opened it, pulled out the paper and began reading it. I looked at the civilian secretary and saw the "Notary" sign behind her. "Will you please notarize this for us and make three certified copies?" I asked.

She looked at the captain who nodded to her; she stamped and signed the paper then made the copies.

I handed one to her. "Please keep this in a file that only you have access to. The others I will take with me and make sure particular people have them."

The captain escorted me into his office and instructed me to sit down as he handed me another paper. "This has your primary contact, mine and a couple of other people's phone numbers. I suggest you find a very safe place for it." He handed me another envelope. "There is five thousand dollars in there. That should get you started and keep you going until you start getting paid from the Blue Note."

He gave me the rest of my instructions and sent me on my way.

After emptying what few things I had in the barracks into my GTO, I loaded the bike on my trailer and headed out the gate.

The first thing I did was go to a lawyer I knew and felt I could trust. I told him the whole story and gave him two copies of the notarized paper and told him we would be talking again in a few days.

Next I headed for the Blue Note bar to meet my new "Boss."

CHAPTER TWO

Finding an apartment in Corpus is no mean feat but finding something half decent with a garage was a task. I finally found an older house that had been pretty well cared for with a detached two-car garage for $120 a month. That was a little steep, but I had to have a safe place for the bike and my GTO. The woman who owned the house was nice, plus she lived in a town about twenty-five miles from Corpus, so I didn't have to worry about her being around much. I paid her for four months rent and that made her much happier. I found a place that rented furniture and got what I absolutely needed and had it delivered.

I knew where the Blue Note was—my folks and I had been there a few times. I don't know why they wanted me to work there. I could have kept working for Louis. I rolled into the parking lot where there were only about four cars parked, and I pulled up as close as possible to the door.

I got off the bike and strolled into the bar. The bar was much as I remembered it, nothing special, though the dance floor looked smaller than I remembered. The gal behind the bar looked at me from top to bottom, "What can I get you?" she asked.

I looked around. "Is the owner around?"

Now she looked at me a little closer. "Yeah, what do you need?"

"I need to talk to him," I said, getting a little irritated. "Where is he?"

"She."

"What?"

"I said 'she.' The owner is a she. Her name is Sherry. Who are you?" she asked.

"My name is TJ Hamlin. She knows who I am," I replied.

She walked from behind the bar and back to a door, knocked and walked in. After a few seconds she walked out followed by a short, attractive redhead. The redhead looked at me and motioned for me to follow her. We walked into a small office with the air conditioner working hard to keep summer on the other side of the door. "Have a seat," she said motioning to a chair.

I sat down and looked at her but before I could say anything she started talking. "I know about your situation, Mr. Hamlin. Someone who knows me very well talked to me about bringing you in here and I agreed; not because I have a lot of trouble in this bar but because I know a little about what they are trying to do, and I am all for it. I don't want drugs in my place if it can be stopped."

I looked at her, "TJ." She looked at me strangely, "Please call me TJ."

This little redhead was living up to the reputation redheads have. Sherry just barely stepped above five feet tall and was a green-eyed knockout. Her body looked like it would be comfortable on a stage but her attitude told me she wouldn't be comfortable there.

"Okay," I told her, "then you probably know more than I do."

"Bullshit! I've heard all about you, TJ. I knew you were in town before your engine cooled down. That's all these suicide jockeys could talk about was you being back. Before I agreed to this thing I was given your complete history, so let's hit an agreement right here and now—you don't bullshit me, I won't bullshit you." Her eyes almost blazed.

I sat there thinking for a minute. "Okay, I am going to take for granted you know everything they could tell you, and it is only fair that you do. The club I belong to is supposedly big into moving meth. I don't know how true it is or how deeply they are involved. I have been asked—no that's not right—I have been ordered...*commanded* to do this and threatened if I don't."

She sat back a little. "That's better. Do you have any idea who is doing what or are you flying blind?"

"Right now I'm flying blind. I don't know who is buying, selling or using. I haven't been in touch with any of my old brothers since I got into town. The only ones I know for sure are still around are Mad Dog and Eddie."

She sat there a minute. "Mad Dog. Is he tall, about six-four, tips the scales somewhere around 250? He looks like a real mean sucker. I know him as Kenny."

I took a quick memory check. "That sounds like Kenny, but he wasn't that big the last time I saw him. He can be a pretty bad number when he is crossed or has had a little too much to drink. Kenny and I were very good friends once. I don't know where we stand now."

She sat there thinking, "Okay, we'll have time to chat later. Let me explain where you stand here; you have the door and keeping order. We don't have trouble often but it will be nice to have someone around if there is any. I know you won't be around all the time but if you can help out on Fridays I would appreciate it—that seems to be the worst day. That's when the guys get paid and come in here to blow their paychecks."

I thought about the bar layout. "So exactly what do you want me to do?"

"TJ, I almost live in this bar and I need a break." The look on her face was serious. "To start, I want you to keep things on an even keel; stop the guys from grabbing at the girls, keep the drunks from raising too much hell, get to know the people who come in and the people who work here. If you are in here any days during the week I may take a little time to get out of this place and away from the smell of beer." She tossed me a set of keys. "You have keys to everything in the place but the safe. If I'm not here at closing, there is a slot you can drop the receipts in."

"You're trusting me with keys and cash? You don't even know me," I said.

She laughed. "You can't run away; I know how to track you down. Now, I am paying you five hundred a week. Well actually I am paying you a hundred; the rest is coming from someone else. For my hundred I really hope you can be here at least Fridays and one other day of the week. I know you have a job to do and this isn't really that job but you could help me a lot."

I looked at her closely for the first time. There was something soft behind that hard shell, something that said she was a lot more than a bar owner. "I will be here every Friday unless it can't be helped, and every night I can during the week, but I promise I will help out at least one day a week. Again, unless something comes up that I can't."

"I've known Jean Marie for a long time and I trust her. She says you are okay. I have to believe her. So I am doing something I don't usually do; I'm trusting you based on a friend and my gut. I usually wait until someone proves they can be trusted." Her face softened a bit. "I don't know what it is, TJ, but there is something that tells me you are different than most of the other men I know."

"Well, I'm not so different than the guys I'm supposed to bust. If I hadn't joined the Navy I might be right where they are, doing the same things they're doing. I will promise you this though; you can trust me, not because the government says so but because I say so."

"Okay, I will introduce you to the day girl, Mindy. She is something of a dip and the only reason I don't think she would steal from me is that she isn't smart enough, but she is a good girl," she said as she got out of her chair and headed for the door.

She introduced me to Mindy, the girl I met when I came in. Mindy was as hot as her name hinted. I am not much of a breast man but hers were beyond belief, that was the first thing I noticed. Then I realized she had long blonde hair, a somewhat pretty face, and a figure that was full enough to indicate she would probably spread out a bit in her later years.

Sherry showed me the rest of the bar. There was a bandstand and on it was a Gibson guitar connected to an amp. I picked up the guitar and plunked out a few notes. She turned on the amp and the sound blared from it.

I twisted through an early Beatles tune, probably missing half the notes.

"Not bad," she said. "Been playing long?"

I smiled. "Since I was ten but I haven't played a whole lot in the past couple of years."

She turned off the amp. "Well, practice a bit; I could use another guitar player. The one I have is a drunk who only shows up when he remembers where his guitar is."

The guitar felt good in my hands. "I'll see if I can find my old Fender. Maybe I can plunk out a couple of tunes. Look," I said, putting the guitar down. "I'll be back in a couple of days—if not before Friday, certainly then."

She put out her hand and I took it. "I'm here to help if I can, TJ. I guess you're part of the family now."

I strolled out the door and headed back to my new digs. I had been putting off calling Eddie but it was time to bite the bullet and do it. I dug out his card and dialed his number.

He laughed. "Well, I'll be damned, you are alive. I thought maybe you fell off the face of the earth. What the hell is the idea of hitting town and not touching base?"

I had to think about how to connect without sounding like I was trying too hard. "Well, a lot has been going on. Leaving the Navy was a real change for me."

"Really? What's that all about?" he asked. I told him the agreed upon story and hoped it sounded true. "Hey, we're going to be at the island this weekend. Come on out and party with us, maybe meet some of the newer guys. There isn't many of the old guard around anymore—everyone turned straight and became citizens," he continued. "How is that old Harley doing? The two brothers that stopped you said you were screaming down the drive."

My Harley was an old one. It was new in 1959 but had been through a number of changes. The latest upgrade was a performance kit that Harley added when the engine was rebuilt and beefed up in

California. "It'll get down the road," I said. "It's more of a Frisco chopper now, no more rigid frame. It's on an Amen Savior frame with a girder front end. Engine is now an 80-incher with a cam that bounces the front wheel at stoplights." The bike really was a screamer; 140-plus was no problem for the nine-year-old machine.

"That's hot, man! I'm driving a brand new machine that has been chopped out, pretty radical for around here. It cost me a bundle but it was worth every dime," Eddie replied.

I wanted to jump in and ask him where he got the money but Eddie was no idiot; he would see right through me. "So, what are you doing these days? Last I heard you were talking about opening a shop."

He laughed a little. "Hell, man, I put that shop up and it went like gangbusters. First year I busted my ass in the shop but after it took off I became management. Man, can you see me as manager?" He laughed again.

"Right, man, you sittin' behind a desk with clean hands? No way," I said.

"I still work on a few of the bikes, mostly for the old guard and do some custom work, but for the dirty shit I let someone else handle it."

"I'm glad things have worked out for you, bro," I told him. "Maybe things will turn around for me."

"So what are you doin'? I heard the Navy let you go. That's a pretty shitty deal, bro. You get your ass shot at for them and they dump you. That really sucks."

"I'm bouncing at the Blue Note; you know the bar out beyond Military run. It isn't a bad gig; the booze is good, pay isn't bad, I have a place to crash, and the chicks that work there give me plenty of eyeball liberty," I told him.

"You know bro, I can always use a good man I can trust in the shop, and I am sure the pay would be better than bouncing," he offered.

I had to think up a good excuse quick. "The pay might be better there, but I bet you don't have any luscious ladies working there. Look, man, I have to cut this off, I need to run. I'll try to make it out to Padre this weekend." I said goodbye and we hung up.

Okay, I had made my first contact with them. I have to admit it felt good to get back to my old friends. I wondered how many friends I would have when this was all over.

I had just poured another cup of coffee when there was a knock at the door; this surprised me since no one knew where I lived. When I opened the door there stood a brown-skinned beauty. She wasn't very tall, 5'2" at most but a wonderfully voluptuous figure. She quickly flashed a badge. "Mr. Hamlin, may I come in please?"

I looked back to her lovely face. "Certainly. Welcome to my humble abode. I guess news travels fast in this town." We walked into the kitchen and I offered her a cup of coffee as she sat down.

"No, thank you, this needs to be very brief. I assume they have told you that you would have a contact within the force. My name is Jean Marie. I will be the only one you will speak to. No one else on the force knows who you are. The only thing anyone will be told is that we have someone on the inside." She handed me a slip of paper. "These are all the phone numbers where you can reach me any time of the day or night."

I took the paper then threw it back on the table, "If I am going to be in this, no one is to know there is someone on the inside. You let *anyone* know there's a rat and people will die. Eventually that someone will be me. Second, this is the last time you come into this house or approach me at all. If you need to talk to me you will call me and we will meet some place where people won't tie the two us together. The same goes if I want to meet with you."

She looked a little flustered but quickly regained her composure. "I take it you don't trust the police department. I can assure you all the people on this task force are completely trustworthy."

"You are either brainwashed, very stupid or one of the best actresses this side of Hollywood. There is no way that drugs could be hitting the streets at the levels I am being told without the assistance of someone inside the police department. So absolutely no one is to know that anyone is on the inside. Does anyone already know? If so I need to check out of this game right now."

"The only one who knows is the Police Commissioner; he was the one who set this thing up. He is also the one who will assign people to the task force and he wanted to meet you. When can we do that?"

"Do you have a hearing problem?" I asked. "Been spending too much time out on the range? Or do you have a problem comprehending my words. I can't speak Mexican so you better take a quick course in English. No one but you is to know I even exist. If I have to say that again I'm walking away, and if I ever find out you leaked my existence to anyone I will drop you so fast you won't remember I was here. Do you have that clear in your mind now?"

I have to admit I was impressed by the way she held her ground. She didn't get in my face, and it was clear she respected where I was but she never backed down either. "You're quite right. I guess I took for granted that we knew what was best, not thinking about the fact that you know a whole lot more about how these people think and operate." She reached in her pocket and pulled out a card, started to hand it to me then pulled it back and looked at it. "I don't suppose it was a good idea to have acquired a concealment privilege for you?"

"Now you are starting to think a little less like a bureaucrat."

She stuffed the card back in her pocket. "I will make sure there is no record of this. Maybe we can start over. I can see we need to work as a team, not with me in the lead."

I smiled. "No, we have accomplished too much to start over. Let's just take this as a learning opportunity and go from here."

"Okay, how can we maintain contact in such a way so as not to arouse suspicion?"

I thought about it for a minute. "There is a mom & pop store on Padre Island Drive named Dave's Bait and Beer. He sells groceries, beer, bait and such. Dave is an old friend—I have even crashed in the back of his store a few times when I was too drunk to make it home. Go in and meet Dave. Don't tell him what you do, just your first name. I'll stop in and talk to him this weekend so he'll know who to look for. If you want to leave anything for me just put it in an envelope and write Lil Brother on it. When there is no one at or near the counter pass it to Dave. If he has anything for you he will pass it to you as well. If the store is too busy, don't hang around; just leave and come back later."

She looked at me concerned. "Are you sure you

can trust him?"

"Definitely! Dave and I have been friends since high school. He has never been a part of the biker scene so he has no ties there. I saved his ass in high school when he stupidly made a pass at a Latina girl and she told her brothers. Two days later her brothers, cousins and everyone who lived in her neighborhood were waiting for Dave when he left school. I happened by and saw there was about to be a serious bloodbath. Fortunately her younger brother was a friend of mine. I apologized for my new friend's stupidity and Dave apologized to Maria. She accepted the apology and the issue was dropped. You know the really crazy thing? That stupid son-of-a-bitch started dating her a month later and they got married when they graduated. So to answer your question, I trust Dave with my life. Just make sure no one sees you there too often, don't stay too long and never leave without buying something. Okay, for now you have been here too long. Meet me at Mike's on North Beach around eleven tonight."

She put her hand out. "I will be there. Thank you."

I took her hand and was surprised to discover she had a firm grip, better than many men I have met. "Don't thank me yet. We are starting down a road we may both wish we had never taken the first step onto."

I escorted her out, went to the fridge and grabbed a bottle of carbonated water and noticed I didn't have much left. I would need to keep a good supply back here to keep me from attacking the booze at the bar.

★ ★ ★

Mike's was a small bar on North Beach, kind of a crummy place, like most everything on North Beach. At one time it was a resort area but over the years it had become run down. It was a great area if you were looking for hookers, drugs or a really cheap roach-infested place to live. The owner, Mike, was another trusted friend—actually he had been my mother's friend but he'd been nice to me since I was a kid. Of course he still seemed to see me as that kid.

Jean Marie showed up dressed much more casually, that is if you can call casual a pair of jeans that looked like they had been painted on and a sweater that made her breasts appear to stand up even prouder. I looked her over. "Damn, honey, you are gonna spoil my bad reputation."

She frowned at me then broke into a smile. "I would slap most men who said that to me, but you actually made it sound like a compliment."

I laughed. "It was a compliment. I'm just glad you weren't dressed that way when you came to the house. You make it hard to concentrate."

She smiled. "Okay, next time I'll wear a gunny sack so I don't distract you. Now, what's good to eat here? I'm starved."

I looked at her appreciably; thinking even a gunny sack couldn't hide her charms and if she ate very much those jeans would explode. "You better like seafood—the fish and shrimp are fresh and excellent, but this guy can turn any steak into shoe leather."

We made small talk as we ate, then we ordered a beer and sat there. "So tell me about these guys," she said. "I know you have been away for a while but tell me what you know."

I leaned forward in my chair, "Okay, let's see.

First there is Eddie. He is the club pres, that's president. Eddie is pretty much old-school biker; he lives to ride, drink, fight and screw in that order, or at least he did before he opened the shop. Last time I saw him, he didn't have two nickels to rub together, and now he seems to be rolling in green. The bike he rides is probably worth twenty grand and it had to cost him a hundred thou to even start up the shop. He hasn't opened up about where he got the cash."

I took a drink and continued. "Then there is Mad Dog, Kenny. He is the enforcer for the club and he loves the job. I don't know much about where he stands now, but I understand from my government contact that he is a major player in the drug scene. That is pretty surprising because I remember him as being pretty straight-laced about drugs…booze, yeah; he would hit that but never drugs. He is a mean son-of-a-bitch drunk or sober. I hate to think what he would be like on meth. Those are the only two I have heard about since I got back to town. Now, I did notice when I ran into a couple of club members, they were carrying guns, something we never did in the past."

She looked at me concerned. "How are you going to get in close enough to find out anything? I seriously doubt these guys are just going to open up."

"You are absolutely right. This is not going to be a brief operation, and results aren't going to come easy. It will take time to build trust," I told her. "The down side is, the longer it takes, the more chance for mistakes but if we rush in they are going to make me and I'm dead. These guys are as bad as they come. When they are crossed they strike back and they strike back hard, doing four times the damage that was done to them. I don't know exactly how I am going to get in close to them, but I know it is going to be a slow process."

She slid a package across the table toward me. "I understand the .45 is your weapon of choice. This one is a customized Colt Combat Commander that has had an accuracy job done to it, adjustable trigger and Rattlesnake grips. The gun is completely clean, no history or records at all. If you need anything else, go to Stan's, the surplus store on Staples and hand them this" —she slid a card across that had one word stamped across it: "Vet" — "The man who runs the place is Stan. You talk about trusting Dave with your life, that is how I feel about Stan. If there is anything you want, just tell him. He will get it and if you need me in a hurry and can't call, just tell him to call J and tell him what you want to pass along."

I took the card. "Thanks, there might be a couple of things I want to pick up."

"TJ, I am more than a little concerned for you," she said seriously. "Do whatever you think is right but if things get too hairy, run like hell. I would rather explain why we failed than bury you."

She really did care about what happened to me. "I know these guys. There are some newbies who I don't know at all, but I think I can deal with them. I have a long history with the club and the old guard will pretty much trust me—they have no reason not to. As for the newer members, I am certain they will be suspicious but the old guys will back me."

We finished our beers and left without saying much more. The ride back felt good, I was back in the saddle, back in my home town and ready to rock and roll. As I rode over the bridge from North Beach I was able to look across the whole city. Somewhere down there, drugs were passing from hand to hand, people were being hurt, people were dying. It was a very sobering thought.

I decided it was a nice night to head for the island, so I pointed the bike in that direction and as soon as I was away from the city proper I rolled the throttle and let the little beast breathe.

I was not quite to the causeway to the Island when I changed my mind and headed for The Cue, the bar where my ex-girlfriend worked and where I suspected I would stumble across some of the brothers.

CHAPTER THREE

The Cue had been a nice pool bar at one time. Now the tables have cigarette burns, beer stains on the felt and the stench of stale beer throughout. Except for the hanging lights over the tables, there was little to brighten the darkness, but my old girlfriend's voice, a sound similar to the screech of a Blue Jay, cut through the darkness so I was able to find the bar. I walked over, sat down and ordered a beer as my eyes became accustomed to the low light. There were at least five CC Riders in the bar shooting pool, then I saw Mad Dog at the back of the bar. Now was as good a time as any to talk to him; I was certain he knew I was in town.

I walked to the back of the bar and up to Mad Dog. "Hey bro, long time."

He looked at me. "I heard you were in town. What are you doing here?"

"Just stopped for a beer," I replied.

He looked at me as though I were a bug. "I mean in Corpus, smart ass. I don't much give a shit why you are in here."

"I got stationed here and this is where I left the Navy, so I decided to hang here for a while."

"What I hear is that you got your dumb ass kicked out. What were you doing, punkin' in there?"

"Mad Dog, I don't want to have to deal with your bullshit, but if I have to I will, and you remember what happened the last time you decided you wanted to dance? Next time I won't be so nice." I turned and started walking away. Some would say it isn't smart to show your enemy your back, but he knew me well enough that he didn't want to jump me.

I walked back to the bar and two of the other bikers came over. "You givin' Mad Dog a hard way to go?"

I picked up my bottle of beer. "Who are you, his wet nurses? Back off unless you want to deal with Eddie."

One of the little punks was stupid enough to open his mouth. "Eddie doesn't run my life, and I see no reason to back off from some punk ass like you."

"I'll be sure to pass your sentiments along to Eddie, and unless you're looking for a little dental rework I suggest you back off," I said, knowing I was goading him. I looked at his friend. "That goes for you too."

They looked at one another then walked away. I finished my beer and walked out.

Once out the door I moved pretty fast, stepped across the bike, cranked it up and blew down the road. After running through some back streets I got back on Padre Island Drive and headed for the Island.

I stopped in at Dave's on my way to pick up a six pack. "Hey Dave, how's it hangin'?"

"Hey TJ. Too low to be used," he said and came out from behind the counter to give me a hug and slap me on the back so hard I almost stopped breathing. "How have you been? It's been a long time."

I thought for a second. "Yepper, a little over three years. I'm doing okay, working a gig at the Blue Note."

"Really? You mean to tell me you get to work around all that sweet stuff down there?" he said in mock wonder.

"Oh yeah, all of it sweet and dangerous," I told him. "Dave, hey, there is a little Mexican gal who might stop in and drop something off for me from time to time. Will you hold on to it until I stop in again?"

"You got it, man, anything you want, you know that."

"Thanks Dave, this is just between us. I don't need to tell you to keep it quiet. How are Maria and the kids?"

He laughed. "Pregnant again, man, pregnant again. It seems like she's been pregnant from the second I said I do. This will make number seven. I have my basketball team. I guess she either wants backups or she is shooting for a baseball team. You better get your ass over to see her. If she finds out you're in town without stopping, she will chase you down and cut off your balls."

"I promise I will stop by as soon as I know it's safe. Look, Dave, I have to be straight. I'm in some pretty tough shit. I can't tell you much about it, only that it could come down hard on me and the less you know the better."

He looked at me concerned. "Hey man, you know I'm here. I will keep it quiet."

"If any of the club come around tell them, yeah, I've been here, long time friends catching up. I won't go see Maria unless I know it's safe, but I will stop by soon," I promised.

He looked at me, knowing not to push the issue. "Okay bro, you know where we live. You know where I am, and you know you are welcome any time. I heard you had some trouble in the Navy, got kicked out or something. Is that true?"

"I'm afraid it is. Now I just have to work things out from here; it's almost like starting over again. I know everything will work out in the long run, but this short run is killing me. I will talk to you later, bro, I have to get on down the trail for now." I shook hands again and headed for the door.

"Keep the shiny side up man, and, hey, you know I am here any time you need me," he said as I walked out the door.

The moon was setting like a small reddish orange ball on the horizon. What was that old saying? Oh yeah, "Red at night sailor's delight, red in the morning, sailor take warning." I wondered if a red moon meant the same thing. I was sure that much of the red came from the pollution we were filling our atmosphere with.

It had been a hot day but the night promised a little cool down, and I figured the best place to be to cool down was the island; that's where all the brothers would be. I pointed my bike toward the causeway and rolled the throttle open, letting the big bike breathe to life, and headed for Padre Island, not sure what I was going to find there. I love the road, particularly with a big engine thumping under me and the wind pulling at my hair. It was times like this when all the troubles in the world were somewhere behind me, and the rest of the world could go to hell.

I heard a sound and looked in my mirrors. A cop determined to ruin my day. I rolled to the side of the road and reached for my wallet as the cop walked toward me.

He looked me over disapprovingly. "Driver's license and registration please," he said in a tired voice.

I was already holding them out and almost made

a smart-assed remark but held my tongue.

"You know, we have speed limits in this state for a reason; they aren't a suggestion, they aren't a minimum, they are the limit at which you may drive this road when conditions are good."

I sat there while he walked back to his car.

A few minutes later he walked back beside me. "Keep your speed down and as soon as you get a chance call Jean Marie," he said as he handed back my cards. He looked at me like I was a bug. "You're lucky, you must have friends somewhere," then he turned, walked back to his car and took off slinging gravel at me as he went.

I have to talk to Jean Marie. She is going to get my ass killed yet, I thought as I started the big machine and rolled my speed past ninety, blowing past the cop who had just stopped me. As long as I was protected I might as well have fun with it.

Padre Island was always the place I felt at peace. I rolled down onto the beach, past Bob Hall Pier and moved further down the island. I pulled up into the sand, took off my vest and set it under the kickstand to prevent it from sinking into the sand and stepped off my bike once I was sure it was safe. I sat there allowing the roar of the engine and the wind to float from my ears and soon had the roar of the waves crashing on the beach replace it. Here I found the kind of peace I could know nowhere else in the world. I felt I was home again for the first time since my return.

I sat there and dozed off for a little while and was startled awake by the sound of a half dozen Harleys passing by. I got up, shook the sand from my vest, brought the engine to life and headed the same direction the bikes had gone.

The party could have been seen by planes flying at 10,000 feet without any problem. There must have been at least seventy-five bikes there, and twenty of them were drag racing in the sand. I stopped and looked up just as a ragged-out Sportster went down, throwing the rider a good twenty feet. The young rider got up spitting sand and cussing the other rider for pushing him into the softer sand. Some dweeb was trying to play "Wild Thing" on an acoustic guitar and butchering the song so bad he should have been arrested by the music police—some people should just enjoy their music in the quiet of a soundproof room somewhere.

Eddie was holding court amongst a dozen bikers, most of them prospects and none of them looked like they knew what a razor was; long hair was the deal but these guys looked more like girls than guys. I couldn't help but think, *where the hell are the new bikers coming from, some kiddy farm?*

I found the beer and popped a top and just strolled around the collection of bikers and their women. Suddenly hands went over my eyes. A body with well-formed breasts pressed against my back and a sweet sounding, "Guess who?" whispered into my ear on beer-dusted breath.

I knew who it was; she was probably the only person who could slip up on me without me knowing she was there. "Shauna," I replied. Shauna was a Native American who came to Corpus on the back of a member's bike when we returned from Sturgis a few years ago and had been hanging around ever since. I turned to her and was a bit amazed by her appearance; though her breasts were still large and firm, her face had aged by decades instead of years.

"Did they finally pass a law allowing you guys to

drink fire water?" I asked.

She smiled at me. "Just beer, dude. I stay away from the hard stuff. It got me into too much trouble."

I couldn't help but wonder what else she was into; she looked like she had been on a meth bender for more than a day or two. I threw my arm around her shoulder, "So, what's been up with you? I see you are still hanging around this bunch of gear heads."

Her eyes were sunken into her head and had lost their shine. Her voice had even gotten a little smoky. "Nothing really, just beatin' around, trying to keep my head above my shoulders. Hey, dude, you don't have any speed or anything on you, do you? I gave up crystal, but I need something to keep the buzz going."

I looked at her hard. "Shauna, you know me better than that. I don't touch that crap and you need to pull off it too. Hell, the booze was bad enough, but this stuff will kill you. When I left here you were having fun, enjoying life…what happened?"

"Bullshit, life sucks and if I don't have something to escape that reality I might as well find a hole to crawl into. Look, TJ, you have no idea what has been going on around here. You better watch your back." Just as she was finishing, Mad Dog came over, grabbed her arm and started dragging her away without a word.

I grabbed him by the sleeve and spun him around. "I was talking to Shauna. I don't appreciate you interrupting us." I was expecting the fist and anticipated it perfectly; he brought in a roundhouse that certainly would have cold-cocked me if it had connected, but he telegraphed every move and I easily avoided his hand. I grabbed his wrist and allowed his own momentum to drive him to the ground, then stepped back. I looked at him as he rose to his feet. "Just back off MD. The last time we did this dance you were out of commission for two weeks. Don't make the same mistake."

He looked at me as though he wanted to kill me. "I'm not the same person anymore, TJ. While you've been playing with your candy-assed boyfriends, some of us have been out here in the real world."

"Looks like you've been in the real world sucking on a bottle and growing a gut," I responded.

I was ready for him when he came. He hadn't changed; he was still the same clumsy, lumbering slob he had always been. MD was a big guy alright; he was 6'6" and around 275 and it wasn't all fat. If he ever really connected with one of his haymaker punches he could do some damage. I easily ducked his swing and caught him in the solar plexus with a sharp, hard punch. I heard the wind go out of him, and he staggered back.

"Come on, MD. You are just going to shame yourself and the colors and have your whole night ruined. Now back off before this gets serious."

The rage in his eyes was still there, and I saw his left hand moving toward his belt; before he could even unsheathe the knife, I had him in the sand face down, his left arm pulled so far up his back that his hand almost reached his collar, and I was pushing up hard. Before he could move I slammed my elbow into his right kidney as hard as I could.

I was going for a third time when Eddie came over. "Okay, children, that's enough fun for tonight. TJ, get off him, and Mad Dog, I think you need to go for a ride and chill your bones a bit. Don't come back until you've cooled down enough to party."

I got up and walked over to Shauna, took her by the arm and walked her away. I watched as MD stepped across his bike, kicked it to life and dumped the clutch causing the bike to twist around in the sand before finally moving down the beach.

Eddie came over to me. "TJ, you better be careful of that one. He thinks you are back here to push him out."

"You know better, Eddie. That is just his excuse to stir up shit. I hate to say it but I think we are going to have issues until one of us puts the other down hard, and I will tell you right now, when the smoke clears I am going to be the one standing, so I suggest you tell him to back off. Next time you might not be around and I might not stop once I get him on the ground." I turned and walked back over to Shauna.

I could tell she was getting in a bad way; she was shaking so bad she could hardly light her cigarette. She finally got it lit and looked at me. "TJ, you know I have always liked you, but Kenny is going to beat the crap out of someone tonight and it scares me."

I looked at her and grinned. "I have no intention of allowing him to my back and that is the only way he is going to have a chance of taking me."

Her eyes blazed. "Not you, dumbass, I mean me. He is going to come back and when we're alone he is going to beat the crap out of me. The last time he got mad at me, after he closed both my eyes and knocked out a couple of teeth, he turned me out to anyone he could find. For three days all I did was spread my legs. I can't go through that again. I won't go through it again. I will end it before that happens."

I could tell she really was scared. "Look, come on over to my place. Stay there until I can talk to him and cool him down. Now that I know what's bothering him, maybe I can get him to chill."

She looked down, tears rolling down her cheeks.

"I'm hurting, TJ. I need a bump real bad. Can you get me something to get me through?"

I didn't like this—the very thing I was supposed to be out here trying to get a line on and I had to go hunting for it. I went to Eddie. "Hey, bro, I need to get my hands on some speed. Who's holding?"

Eddie looked at me warily. "I didn't think you were into drugs, man. I thought you were clean."

I just looked at him. "It isn't for me. Shauna is hurting and I take it MD has her stuff. Just tell me who's holding."

The frown on his face relayed his thoughts. "You are getting in over your head. Kenny has a half dozen riders he can call on, and he will do that if he can't beat your ass himself. Now you are messing with his old lady. That is as dumb as I have ever seen you. The whole damned club could come at you for that."

"I'm not messing with Shauna. She is scared to death that he's going to beat her again. She says he beat the crap out of her and made her pull a train. It sounds to me like he is over the edge."

An awkward smile went across his face. "Yeah, I've seen her on more than one occasion after he tuned her up, but she is his old lady and it is none of your business. In the end she will run back to him no matter what he or anyone else says or does. She's a meth head—she lives for that shit and nothing is going to change that. I tell you, TJ, ever since that stuff has hit the club we have more guys using. At first they just cooked and sold it. Now they're using as well. If you take her with you, there will be a dozen pissed bikers on your trail. Leave her alone, get on out of here, and I will do the best I can to take care of her."

I turned and looked over at Shauna. She was standing next to another biker, and from the looks of it, she was getting fired up. She didn't even look my way as I got on the bike and headed down the beach in the same direction Kenny had.

CHAPTER FOUR

As I tripped down the beach I just wanted to sit down with Kenny and talk, explain to him I wasn't trying to make a move on his property, not trying to take his place in any way. Kenny and I used to be the best of friends, where when you saw one of us the other was close by. If you got into it with one of us, we would both be on your ass. I even gave up on one girl when we were in high school because Kenny had it bad for her. We had partied together, tripped down to Mexico venturing into Boy's Town to party together. We fought our way out of more than one bar, watching each other's backs. I guess we were as close as any brothers could be, but somewhere along the line there was a sudden and violent split.

I saw his headlights bouncing down the beach and pulled over, hoping he would stop and we could talk away from the others. He blew past me, though, staring at me as his bike thundered by. I turned the bike around, not certain now whether I was going to stop or just keep going and look for another day. As I got closer to the party, I saw four bikes and riders sitting there idling; one of those riders was Kenny. As I cruised by, the four bikes pulled in behind me coming up close to my taillight. When the lead bike gave me a gentle nudge, I rolled the throttle as hard as I dared on the hard packed sand. Then I saw a fifth rider up ahead. I rolled the throttle hard, no longer taking any care about my traction.

I aimed the bike for the fifth rider up ahead, hoping I could get him to pull out, but he was either stoned or ballsy because he held his line. I tube-locked the throttle now, screaming through the gears, the big eighty-incher pegging the tach in each gear.

I was pulling far enough ahead of the other riders that they couldn't pen me in. Just before I reached the front bike I was in fifth gear and pushing 135 on the sand, praying nothing went wrong. The rider was evidently relieved with my decision not to kill us both but now he was trying to make up ground. I knew I was going to have to slow when I got to Bob Hall Pier and just hoped I could build enough cushion before I got there. As the packed sand veered to the left toward the asphalt road, it also seemed to soften, causing the bike to slow rapidly. This didn't bother me because the looser sand would have the same effect on the other bikes.

I hit the blacktop and let the big engine have its head. By then I was pushing about my top speed at a little over 160, and as hard as they tried the other bikes began to fade. When I hit the causeway I dumped my lights and headed for the curve that would take me to Dave's bait shop. After I got through the curve, I got on the brakes hard, fighting to keep the bike upright and my ass off the pavement.

When I was right in front of Dave's, I laid the bike hard over, nearly losing it as I hit the parking lot, and dipped behind the shop. The five bikes blew past Dave's and kept going. A few miles down the road I saw the reds from a state cop flash on, roll for a ways then give up the chase.

I stashed the bike behind the bait shop and walked in the back door.

When Dave saw me he smiled. "Short party?"

I grabbed a beer out of the cooler, popped the top and walked up front and dropped a single in front of him. "Yeah, short party. It seems Kenny has a hard on for me; he wants to make me his personal punching bag."

He laughed. "His personal punching bag? Last time you two got into it he pissed blood for three days. That hard head is a waste of bad air."

"Well, I'm afraid he isn't alone," I said.

He looked toward the front window. "Was that them that blew past here just before you came in?"

Taking a hard knock on my beer I looked out the glass. "Yeah, that was him. Look, I better get out of here. I don't want him stopping and finding me here. Look, if he stops don't lie to him. Just tell him I was here, had a beer and split."

He frowned. "Look, TJ, you know I don't have to tell him that."

I started toward the back door. "No, don't lie to him. All he has to do is follow my tracks to the back, and he will know you weren't telling the truth. Then you are in trouble with him, and your old lady will kick my ass."

"She will kick your ass anyway if she hears you call her my old lady. So, what happened with you guys? The two of you were thick as thieves."

I opened the back door and stepped through. "It's a long story. Maybe we can sit down with a couple of longnecks and chew it over. For now, I need to get out of here before Kenny comes back this way."

"Hey, I almost forgot," he yelled as I headed out the door. "Your Mexican chick stopped in about an hour ago. She says she really needs to talk to you."

I fired up the panhead and sat there thinking for a minute trying to decide where to go; I didn't want to head for the apartment—that would be one place they would look if they knew where it was. I looked at my watch, still had two hours before I needed to be at the bar but that was probably the safest place.

As I was pulling out onto Padre Island Drive I remembered a place I really did need to go. I took the drive for a few miles then dropped into surface streets trying to keep out of sight and headed for North Beach. I knew Kenny wouldn't think about looking for me there; I headed down Staples, through Five Points and past the "T" heads where some of the nicer boats were tied up. Over the bridge and down into some of the seedier parts of North Beach to a place few people knew about. Blasters was an old rundown bar with floors so weak the pool table had to constantly be leveled, but it was a place I knew I could find what I needed.

The darkness of the bar made it impossible to see anything for a few minutes. This served to give the people inside the bar the opportunity to bail out if the cops came in. From behind the bar came Carl's booming voice. "Well, butter my butt and call me a biscuit. I thought you was dead."

I was finally able to see the gray-haired old man, and I strolled over to the bar. "There are a few people who thought so and even more who wished it was true."

He started to go for a longneck, and I stopped him. "C'mon, man, you have some of that good stuff, don't you?"

He laughed, reached under the bar, pulled out an unmarked bottle and poured the clear liquid into a glass. "If that stuff don't kill ya, it will cure ya."

I poured about half the 12-ounce glass of fire down my throat and fought back a cough and the desire for a glass of water to chase it. "Damn," I said, "life just got a hell of a lot better."

After that I just sipped at it. I looked around; the nearest people to me were four old guys playing dominoes. "Carl, I need something like a 380. Something small but good enough at close range. It's got to be clean, nothin' behind it, no history."

He looked at me concerned. "You in some kinda trouble, man?"

I thought for a heartbeat; this old man was as good as they come and there wasn't anybody going to come after him. "I could be. I really don't want to tell you any more, but yes, I could be and carrying my Colt around is pretty hard, too easy to see."

He served another customer at the end of the bar then walked back to the little storage room that served as an office, coming out shortly with a paper bag that he set on the bar. "They are Walther PPKs, just got my hands on a couple a few days ago. Take them both; there are four extra clips and a box of hot loads. You didn't get them here."

Without looking in the bag I stuffed it in my cutoff. "What do I owe you?"

"They cost me 150 each, just cover that and we will call it even. If you don't have it with you, drop it off when you can," he said.

I pulled out four one hundred dollar bills and laid them on the counter as I knocked back the rest of my drink and headed for the door. "I didn't get them here, gotcha man."

I got on my bike and pointed it back to town. North Beach was once a hangout for my mother and stepfather, that's how I got to know the place, and old Carl had been a part of the scene down there as far back as I could remember. Now North Beach was long past its glory days, but there were still some good people there, people you could depend on.

Back on the road and over the bridge I headed toward the Blue Note. The warm night air caressing my face was like the touch of an old lover. On the road I always felt good, felt like it was where I belonged. I often thought this must have been the way early cowboys felt on a cattle drive; out in the wind, nobody to hassle them, everything they were responsible for right there in front of them. It was a feeling I longed for. At that moment I wanted to turn the bike around and just disappear and never look back. I wondered how long I could run before someone came along and dragged me back.

I cruised on out to the Blue Note and dropped into the caliche parking lot before I noticed Kenny's bike. None of the other bikes were there so I parked right next to his, dropped one of the 380s in my waist band, took the .45 out of my belt and dropped it in the bag then walked in the front door. Crystal was behind the bar, and I ordered a Coke as my eyes adjusted to the dark room. Crystal was a sweet little fox, light brown hair, large blue eyes and a figure that would drop you to your knees; add to that a voice so sweet and sexy it melted butter. As I picked up my Coke I slid the bag containing the other guns and spare mags across to her. "Stick this where it will be safe."

She took the bag without looking inside and dropped it in one of the coolers then looked across the room behind the pool tables. "That guy back there has been asking about you."

I could barely make Kenny out through the smoky room and the darkness. I kept looking at him but talked to Crystal. "Look, if trouble starts, get Hank off his ass and send him over." Hank was a burly trucker, hell of a nice guy but not someone you wanted pissed at you. His arms were as large as my legs, and only the slightest bit of a beer belly kept him from looking like he should be in body building competitions.

I walked across the room to the booth Kenny was sitting in. "You lookin' for me?" I asked.

He looked up at me, pointed at the seat across from him. "Sit down, bro. We need to talk before one of us gets hurt."

I sat down, never taking my eyes off his. "I am a little uncomfortable sitting here when I can't see both your hands," I said as I made sure mine were on the table.

He nodded and brought both hands up to pour his beer. "That's cool, I can do that."

I still hadn't taken my eyes off his. "So, what is so important that you have to chase me all over town? Last time I saw you and your cronies, you didn't look like you were in the mood for conversation."

"C'mon, bro, I couldn't let you slap me around then just walk away. I had to make a show. Hell, I knew I wasn't catching that machine of yours. You blew us off like we weren't even in town. Where the hell did you go anyway?"

"Just cruisin' around." I certainly wasn't going to tell him I had stopped at Dave's place. "So, what's on your mind?" I asked as I finally allowed my eyes to drift from his.

"Look, this thing between you and me gotta stop. Like I said, one of us is gonna get hurt or worse," he said taking a drink of his beer.

I really felt like hurting him, just beating him into the ground. "It's not just about you and me anymore. You slappin' Shauna around and turnin' her out like you did, that's pretty shitty. I always thought you were more of a man than that," I growled.

"TJ, you saw her. She was so strung out it wasn't even funny. I am tired of being her supply line when she needs something, then just a bank when she can get it from me. Yeah, I turned her skinny ass out. She needs to learn to pay for what she gets, and that was my way of collecting. As for tuning her up, you're right, that was really wrong. No matter how big a pain in the ass she is."

I lit a cigarette and sat back, thinking, then called Crystal over. "Bring us two doubles from the bottle under the bar."

Kenny had a wondering look on his face when Crystal brought two on the rocks glasses filled with amber liquid. "Okay, Kenny," I said, "we start clean from here, but understand that if I see you mistreating Shauna again, it's on. Take it down." We knocked glasses then emptied them in one swallow.

He looked at me, eyes watering, "Okay, we're cool. I'm heading out. Wanna ride?"

"Can't, I got the door and floor tonight. Kenny," I said, watching his eyes, "don't get me wrong, I don't want to fight you, I don't want the tension between us, and I hear what you're saying, I just don't know if I trust it. I mean you go from blood in your eyes to mister nice guy doesn't click with me."

He sat there for a minute. "TJ, I have some problems, some issues I am working through. Shauna is one of those issues. I introduced her to speed, but it was just supposed to be for fun. Now she is on meth and I can't deal with her. It scares me."

I wasn't sure what to believe. "But you are her supplier. You are the one getting the stuff for her. I can't help it, man. There is something rotten here, and

I can't put my finger on it."

He looked me straight in the eyes. "Do you remember the days, TJ? The days when we rode and raised a little hell; when we used to make runs down to Mexico to party and pick up a little grass or speed? Man, those were the days. Remember the year we got a wild hair and took off to Sturgis when the run was a couple hundred hard core riders? Those days are gone, man, those days are history. The club is changing, everything is changing."

I smiled at the memory of those days. "Yeah, man, I remember. That first trip to Sturgis was something else. The townies didn't care much for us and we damned near ended up in jail, but it was a blast."

He frowned. "It ain't there no more, man, it's gone. Now everything is about taking care of business. And don't let Eddie fool you—he is at the top of this thing."

I looked at Kenny, wondering if he was putting me on. "What thing? What the hell are you talking about?"

I could see the rage coming into his face. "Meth. For the last two years, all Eddie thinks about is cooking meth and selling it. There are people working around the clock cooking and packing the stuff. That has torn this club apart; in fact it isn't a club any more, it's a business."

I could see Kenny was down but there wasn't much I could do about it right now. "Look, sit here and finish your drink. I have to get on the door before the girls start. Just chill for a while."

I left Kenny there and went to the door. "Crystal, keep an eye on my friend, will you? Let me know when he leaves if he goes out the back."

She smiled at me. "Sure, TJ, but it'll cost you."
I smiled back at her and thought, *That is a debt I would love to pay.*

CHAPTER FIVE

It was about 9 o'clock when it started getting busy in the club and about the same time that Kenny walked toward me as I checked identification at the door. He grabbed my right hand. "I'm heading out, bro; the party at the beach should be firing up pretty good by now."

"Okay, bro, keep it between the ditches and stay cool," I replied.

"I will. I need to talk to Shauna, but she is pretty pissed at me right now. TJ, how the hell am I going to get her off that stuff, man? It is all over the place and way too easy to get her hands on."

"I don't know, Kenny, I really don't, but maybe we can talk about it later. For now, just chill out and try to relax for the weekend. Maybe after that your head will be clear enough to find some of the pieces and get them in place."

He nodded. "Maybe you're right. Maybe I just need to keep my mind off it for a while. I will see you a bit later. Please try to make it out to the island."

I assured him I would be out there some time over the weekend and returned to checking IDs.

This was my first real day to work at the club, and I didn't know what to expect. It was about thirty minutes before the crowds started showing up, and the music was getting louder and louder. At 9:30, the first dancer hit the stage.

She went by the name Sweet Candy and she was

all her name hinted at. Her real name was Wanda Lee, which was one reason she went by Sweet Candy—to everyone else her name was Lee. Just as Lee started dancing, I saw three bikers coming toward the door; I couldn't tell whether they were Rider members or not from the front, but they were definitely bikers.

"Hey, bro, you're TJ right?" the largest of them spoke, offering his right hand.

I grabbed his hand, "Yeah, brother, what's up?"

He smiled and looked back at the other two. "I'm Casper, been with the club a couple of years. Just up for a little partying before we head out to the island. Heard you might be here and knew you wouldn't turn a brother away."

"I remember you. I would never turn away a brother who is old enough to drink," I replied.

He looked at me as if he could cut me with his eyes. "They're brothers, man, you can't turn them away. They're old enough to fly the colors, they're old enough to drink."

"Sounds good to me," I said, "but the state of Texas doesn't agree. Now, any of you who are twenty-one can come on in. The others will have to wait until they get to the island."

Casper got right in my face. "You're an asshole, you're not a brother. This ain't over. You get your ass out to the island and we'll settle this. You don't treat a brother this way. Eddie will deal with you when I'm through."

I stepped forward enough to make Casper back up. "You take your ass along with these kids and get out of here before I embarrass you in front of your little boys."

He pushed at my chest and backed off. "I'm going to enjoy kicking your ass," then he walked away with his two friends.

I turned to walk back into the club, but three large men stood in front of the door. I looked up at them. "Show's over, gents. Let's get back inside before the girls think we would rather stand around looking at one another."

The rest of the night was uneventful at the club; oh sure, I had to tell a couple guys to keep their hands off the girls, but I had expected that, you can't expect red-blooded American boys to look and not touch. Soon after the girls left the stage and last call was made, the place started getting empty. I went around and cleared off the tables and helped the girls get the trash out. Then Sherry called me back to the office. I was surprised to see Jean Marie sitting at Sherry's desk. "Do you think it is a good idea to be around here?" I asked.

She sat a little forward. "Sherry and I have been friends for years, and I come and go from here quite often, she even gave me a key so I could get in the back door. No one is going to think it strange for me to be here."

"It still bothers me, three of the guys from the club tried to get in here but at least one was underage so I sent them on their way. Of course now I'm going to have to deal with Casper when I get to Padre but I knew there was going to be trouble with him sooner or later," I told her.

"Casper. That name rings a bell. I'll check on him when I get back to the office. Did you get the names of the other two?" she asked.

"No, and I didn't recognize them. Look, Jean Marie, everything I've heard about Kenny tells me he is deep into this meth business. Is it possible everyone has him wrong?" I asked.

Jean Marie thought a moment then shook her head. "I'll look into that, too. I don't remember anyone from the surveillance teams saying anything about him. No, wait, I do remember one of the teams saying something about him giving one of the women meth."

"Surveillance teams? Do any of them know who I am?" I asked.

She laughed. "TJ, please stop doubting me. You made it perfectly clear about things like that. No one has been told anything about you. No one except me knows anything about you, and I'm working hard to make sure no one knows we have someone undercover."

"I'm sorry, I really am starting to sound paranoid, but I just don't know who I can trust; I don't know who is involved in what, and I am more than a little concerned. Other than you, no one has my back, and I can't relax for more than a minute," I said.

"TJ, Sherry can be trusted and you have your friend Dave, so there are at least three in your corner."

"Three; that is a pretty small army to fight something this large," I answered.

"Well, three is what we have, so we will go with three, at least for now. Don't get in a hurry, TJ. It may take a while to get what everyone wants and if we take anything but small steps we could blow the whole thing and get someone hurt," she said.

I reached into the small fridge in Sherry's office, pulled out a bottle of beer and opened it on my belt buckle. "Okay, I will try to calm down and take it slow. It just seems that everywhere I turn I don't see anyone around I can trust." I took a long pull on the beer. "I guess I better get out to Padre. Casper is going to be chompin' at the bit to get his hands on me, and Kenny is expecting me."

"TJ, be careful. It sounds like someone could have you in their sights. I don't think it is because anyone knows anything, but maybe they expect you to try to take a position in the club," she suggested.

I downed the rest of the beer. "They are right. It is what everyone suspects or expects, and if I don't I will draw a lot more attention to myself. I was one of the first members of this club, one of the Dirty Dozen; for me *not* to expect a position in the club would be the wrong way to go."

Jean Marie and Sherry both looked at me, but it was Sherry who spoke. "TJ, I don't know you well, but Jean Marie says you're on the level and that is good enough for me. I don't want to see you hurt either." She set the bag with the other 380 and my .45 on the desk. "You best take this with you," then she got up to walk out.

I dropped the little gun in my back pocket and the clips in my shirt then handed her the .45. "Tuck this away until I can take it to the house." She took the heavy gun and put it in her safe before leaving the office.

"Small fire power," Jean Marie said.

"Yes, but fire power doesn't do a lot of good if everyone can see it. I needed something I could more easily conceal," I said. "Look, I am heading out to the island. On my way I'm going to stop at Dave's. I will touch base with him before he closes on Sunday. If you don't hear from me, check with Dave; if Dave doesn't hear from me, have someone check Padre."

"TJ, you're scaring me. What do you think is going to happen?"

"I don't have a clue, but I know there are more

than a few people who are going to come my way," I said as I turned and walked out the door, through the bar and out to my bike.

The big panhead rumbled to life; it was the only thing in my life that I knew I could depend on. I twisted the throttle and felt the machine leap forward as I ran her through the gears until I reached about ninety, then just kicked back and allowed the wind to start blowing all my issues into the wind currents behind me.

Banking into the turns I pushed the Harley harder blowing through them smoothly. I kicked my speed up as I approached the next turn. Halfway through the turn I could feel the bike slipping just a little. When I came out the other side of the turn, my heart was thumping and a rush of adrenaline flowed through me. This was when I was alive, this was when I knew what I was meant to do; the rest of life was just filler until I could get back into the saddle. The next turn came up fast; it was a tight left and I had to throw the bike across the opposite lane and slowly drift up as I came out of the left turn and on to the straight. I glanced at the speedometer—the needle was passing one-thirty. I backed off and made the turn toward Padre Island Drive then headed for Dave's.

I pulled around to the back, walked in the back door and to the cooler for a beer. I walked up to the counter and threw down a five. "What's up, bro?" Dave asked.

"Same old, same old. Heading out to the island for the party," I told him.

"TJ, man, I don't know what you're into but I'm afraid for you. I know who you're messin' with, and I know as well as you do what happens if you cross them."

"Dave, the only thing I will tell you, the only thing I *can* tell you, is that I don't have any choice in the matter. I am between a rock and a hard place. I just don't have a hell of a lot of choice."

"You always have a choice, isn't that what you always told me? TJ, what can I do to help you? You can't be the only one on this journey. You can't go it alone."

"Even if I could involve you, even if you could be of help, I wouldn't let you. You have a wife and kids to take care of and I'll be damned if you are going to risk that. Look, just be here, do what we talked about. That will be a great help."

Dave looked down then back up to me. "Whatever you need, anything, you know that."

I took a pen and a piece of paper and wrote Jean Marie's private number down. "I'm heading out to the party on the island. I told Jean Marie I would stop by and check in with you on my way back. If I don't stop in here by the time you close tomorrow, call her and tell her you haven't heard from me."

He took the paper and I could tell he was not happy. "You got it. I'll be here all night if I have to. I'll be here until I hear from you."

"C'mon, Dave, you don't have to do that."

"TJ, you have always been there for me. I don't know what's up but I'm here all the way. I'll be here Sunday until you come through. No more arguments."

In the years I had known Dave I had only known him to stand hard against someone or for something a few times. The last one was his wife—he was willing to take a beating if that was what it was going to take to get her to go out with him. He had that same look on his face now. "Thanks Dave. I'll try to get back through here early."

Back on the bike, I headed south toward the island. I ran hard until I got to the beach then kept it slow, just rumbling down the hard packed sand. I could see the party long before I got there; there must have been a dozen fires lighting the skies. I intentionally looked for Kenny's bike and parked next to him.

I wasn't even off the bike when Kenny walked up. "TJ, you better watch your back, man. Casper is running his mouth and is looking for you, says he is going to kick your ass."

I stepped off the bike and started guiding Kenny away from the gathering. "Kenny, I need to ask you a few questions and I really need you to be straight with me. Will you do that?"

Kenny looked at me. "Look, man, I know we got off on the wrong foot, but I'm here, man. I got your back."

"Okay, that answers one question, and that had better be the truth. My other question is about Shauna; are you supplying her drugs?"

The look on his face was pained. "TJ, what the hell am I supposed to do? If I don't, someone else will. At least I might be able to keep her from overdoing it."

"How did she get started then?" I asked.

He looked at the ground. "It was just fun, man; just a little buzz now and then. We went on a run to Natural Bridge and she hooked up with some other women. Next thing I know she is flying high. Ever since then she has been at meth every chance she gets."

"Have you been selling it, making it, anything?" I probed.

"Get real, TJ. I don't even use any more. I have seen too many people get screwed up on this stuff. The last thing I would do is sell or use it. Why, man, what's up?"

"We can talk about that later. I just needed to know about Shauna. I had heard you were her supplier and that you were involved in cooking up the stuff, maybe even selling it. I need to know."

Just then I saw Casper and his two little friends standing next to Eddie and looking our way. "Kenny, are you sure you are ready to back me?"

His eyes moved in the direction I was looking, "Let's get it, bro. I will follow you in."

I walked toward Eddie and Casper. "Okay, shit for brains, I'm here. You have something to say?"

Eddie looked at Casper. "You have a beef with TJ?"

"This piece of shit made me look bad in front of two brothers," he snarled.

Eddie looked at me, "What's up, TJ?"

"This punk shows up at the Blue Note wanting me to let him in with his two children here and I refused to let them in if they were underage." I looked back at Eddie. "When did the club start letting high school kids in our doors?"

"This doesn't sound like club business, sounds like a personal beef. You two are going to have to settle it on your own." He looked at Casper. "Take this shit away from me, get out of here."

Casper walked away with his two boys in tow.

"TJ, you have a right to take one of the officer spots from anyone below your station," Eddie said. "Have you been thinking about that?"

"What does Casper hold?" I asked with a smile.

I could see the smile drift across Eddie's lips.

"Membership. That isn't a very high slot, TJ, but if that is what you want..."

"I hadn't really thought about it, but I think that office needs some strength. Right now it's being run by a wimp. I want it," I told him.

"It's yours. I'll tell Casper," he said.

"Don't bother, Eddie, I'll take care of it," I told him as I started to walk away.

"I had a feeling you were going to say that. Mind if I watch?" he asked, the smile getting broader.

I walked over to where the three of them were standing by the fire. Casper turned quickly as one of his boys said something to him. As I was walking I slipped the two pistols from my waistband and pocket, passing them to Kenny. Casper was standing ready.

"Casper, you just lost your position in the club," I told him. "You have just been sent back to the pack."

I could see the rage building on his face. "So you can run it? No way in hell. Tell him, Eddie. I paid you for this job."

"Yeah, TJ, he did. Then again I never said I was going to change the rules. TJ has a right to the position if he wants it and, quite honestly, I can't do anything about it," he told Casper.

By now there were forty people standing around watching us. Casper turned to me. "Well, I can. I am challenging you for this position. The only way you can take it is to put me down."

"Casper, just walk away. You don't want to do this," I told him.

"Oh, hell yes I do," he said. "You and I both know the reputation you have is all a lie; you are supposed to be so bad and we both know better."

"As usual you are trying to talk me to death," I

said, watching his eyes carefully.

It didn't surprise me a bit when he made a run for me; I stepped to the side and rammed my fist into his right kidney. I laughed hard as he stumbled to the ground and scrambled to his feet. "C'mon, Casper, stop embarrassing yourself," I said, knowing it would infuriate him.

He walked toward me and just before he got to me someone grabbed my arms, allowing Casper to bury his fist in my stomach then across the side of my head with his left fist. My arms were released. I fell to the ground hurting, and my head was spinning. Before I could find my feet, Casper kicked me in the chest, but I managed to grab his foot and roll enough to pull him to the ground.

Casper outweighed me by at least fifty pounds. I struggled to get on top of him but his weight and strength worked for him. He caught me on the side of my face with his fist then wrapped his hands around my throat and began tightening his grip. I managed to grab his thumbs and pulled hard. That loosened his grip and I could hear one thumb crack. When he let go of my throat, I drove my stiffened fingers at his windpipe; this was enough for him to roll away from me.

I got to my feet and gave him time to get to his feet before I came around with a kick that caught him just below the left ear. That was enough to stun him, but he went for the knife on his belt. A roundhouse punch landed hard against the right side of his jaw. He was done then, but I was pissed and I wasn't. I aimed my right heel for the inside of his right knee, and I kicked as hard as I could. He crumbled to the ground.

I walked over to him and ripped his cutoff from

his body. "As the officer of this club responsible for membership, I am removing your colors. The only way you get them back is by proving you are a true brother and being sponsored by a member in good standing," I said as I turned and walked away.

I heard the shot and spun around in time to see Kenny ripping a small auto from Casper's hand. Someone screamed and I saw Shauna falling. Kenny and two others ran to her before I could even move. I kicked Casper hard enough in the face to turn out his lights. I ran over to where Shauna lay. The small caliber round had caught her in the side. Someone drove a truck over so Shauna could be loaded into the back; Kenny and two others got in the back and took off.

I walked over to Casper's two friends. "Give me your patches. You'll get them back when a member in good standing sponsors you for membership and you have prospected until you are voted in. If you don't want to do what is required, get out of here and stay away from any club gatherings. For now, why don't you take your friend to the hospital. I think his leg may be a little hard for him to walk on."

I walked up to Eddie. "What the hell is going on? I don't see many of the old guard. What I do see is a bunch of punk-assed kids and Mexicans. What's going on?"

"TJ, things have changed. Come by the clubhouse tomorrow and we'll talk. This isn't the time or place. Look, let's get back to the party."

I looked around—there was really no one I knew. "I'm not in much of a party mood and I haven't had much sleep. I'm going home. I'll see you tomorrow."

I stepped across the bike and headed down the beach and out to Dave's.

CHAPTER SIX

I was exhausted as I drove across the causeway on the way to Dave's place. I felt like I had been working for three days without sleep. The lights of Dave's shop were like a haven in the middle of hell. I rolled around back and strolled into the shop, dropping in a chair behind the counter. "You look like shit, TJ."

"It sure is nice to know I still have friends willing to be honest with me, maybe a little too honest," I said as I leaned back in the chair and told him about the night's events.

"You need some down time, man. You need to just blow away from everything for a few days," he said with real concern in his voice. The idea sounded good. I didn't have anything special going on, but I couldn't leave without seeing Shauna.

"I think I will just head for home and grab a few hours then run up and see how Shauna is doing, I am sure Kenny is a mess right now," I told him. Then something came to me. "Kenny is going to go looking for Casper. I can't let that happen."

"Why not? It sounds like Casper won't get anything he doesn't deserve," he said.

"You don't know Casper. He got his name because he tends to just suddenly be there; he is a sneaky bastard. Not only that but he is also mean as a snake and not near as predictable."

"So, should I tell your friend you came by?"

I thought for a minute. "Yeah, tell her I will be going to the hospital in the morning as soon as they will let me in. We might be able to talk there."

I got up, got to the bike and turned it toward home. As I pulled onto my street I noticed a car around the corner from the house that I didn't recognize. It was a new car, and this neighborhood was not exactly a high rent district. I cruised by the house then went around the block; there were two men sitting in the car, cops no doubt. I pulled into the garage and tossed my guns into a cabinet after I closed the door and walked into the house. I had just opened a beer when they banged on the front door.

I walked to the front door and asked who it was.

"Corpus Christi Police Department."

I cracked the door and told them to prove it. They showed me their creds, and I swung the door open.

"Are you Thomas Jefferson Hamlin?" asked the fat slob in his wrinkled suit.

I felt like smacking the piggish bastard but knew that would get me nowhere. "Yes," I replied, "but you can call me Mr. Hamlin."

"I am Sergeant Kellum. He's Sergeant Dawson," the other cop said. He was dressed in a suit that actually fit him. "Can we come in and talk for a moment? It seems you may have been a witness to something that happened on Padre Island this evening." Since he acted like a real human being, I allowed them to come in and took them to the kitchen so we could sit down.

"I would offer you a beer but I doubt you would violate the rules by joining me," I chided.

Fatso replied, "No, we are on duty, and we don't drink with suspects."

I looked back at him. "Do you have a warrant?"

"No, but…" he stopped and the other man spoke up. "Mr. Hamlin, you aren't a suspect, and if you become uncomfortable with the questions, we can go downtown where you can call a lawyer."

I knocked down the rest of the beer. "I am already uncomfortable, so why don't you just do that. Take me downtown, and I will call my lawyer, because I have already said all I'm going to. So either put me in your car or get the hell out of my house, because short of goodbye I have said all I will say." I stared at the overweight cop in the crumpled suit then got up and walked to the door and opened it.

"Mr. Hamlin," Sergeant Kellum said, "you are making this harder than it has to be. You witnessed a shooting tonight, and we need to know what you saw."

I looked back at the slob and said, "Goodbye."

"This isn't over," said the nasty looking cop as he walked toward the car at the corner.

I locked the door, glad to have these intruders away from me. I looked out the blinds to see them talking to another cop in a marked police car. *Great*, I thought, *now I have a babysitter*.

I quickly forgot about my recent guests and headed for the shower. The hot water stinging my body began to relax muscles I wasn't even aware were tense. Standing in the shower I tried to get everything clear in my head, but it all seemed to be bouncing in different directions; nothing connected.

It seemed like a week since my head had been on a pillow, and I expected sleep to take me quickly, but I lay there with all these random thoughts screaming through my head. I finally fell asleep and slept until the sun began blasting through the window and burned holes through my eyelids.

After getting a pot of coffee going, I called the hospital to check on Shauna only to find she had left some time during the night. After I hung up I opened the blinds so I could see the street. Soon our friendly neighborhood cop drove by, and I marked the time. I called Kenny. "Hey, bro, I just talked to the hospital and was told Shauna was no longer there."

"I know, TJ, she showed up here about six-thirty this morning. She gave them the name Edwards so they don't have a clue where to look for her," he told me.

"How is she?"

"The bullet was a small caliber and didn't hit anything major. They removed it and put her on antibiotics. The question is, where is Casper?"

"I don't know, Kenny, I left right after you did."

"He's a dead man, TJ. I'm going to find him and take him apart," he said, the rage building in his voice.

"Kenny, leave this alone," I said. "I know you want Casper, and I don't blame you a bit, but this isn't the way. Look, leave it alone. Give me a chance to run him down. We need to talk, but not over the phone and not right now."

"Hey, TJ, I can't let Casper get away with this. First because of Shauna and second because I have to face the rest of the club. I can't do that until I get him," he said with a shaky voice.

I had to find the right words. "Kenny, chill for a couple of days. Take care of Shauna. If I don't have Casper by then I'll help you take him down, but I need some time."

The phone was silent for a long time. "TJ, if it was anyone else I would tell them to go pound sand.

Okay, I will stand down for now, but I won't wait long."

"Okay, I'll be in touch in a couple of days. Don't do anything at all until you hear from me," I said as we said our goodbyes.

I knew I didn't want to hang around where the locals could find me easily so I decided I needed a day or two out of town. I sat in my living room drinking the hot coffee and continued to time the patrolman. It was a clear fifteen to twenty minute pattern, so I would have little trouble getting out of the neighborhood without being spotted. I loaded a backpack with some essentials and went back to the living room.

As soon as the patrol went by, I scooted out to the garage, opened the door and stepped out to see if the cop was around. Not seeing him I pulled the bike out of the garage and headed north.

Fifteen minutes later I pulled down on North Beach and went to Blasters to grab a meal. I used Carl's phone and called Jean Marie. I told her where I was and asked if she could meet with me; she told me she would be there in twenty minutes. It was more like forty-five, and I was through with my meal and hitting my fourth cup of coffee.

"What's up, TJ? I am more than a little surprised you called me," she said.

"Do you know two cops named Kellum and Dawson?" I asked.

She ordered a cup of decaf. "Sure, they are a couple of sergeants assigned to investigate the shooting at Padre Island. I take it they came to see you."

"Yeah, and I don't trust them, well, the fat one anyway," I told her.

"TJ, you should have just told them what you know; they have a job to do and you have some of the answers they need," she said.

"I don't know a damned thing. Shauna was accidentally shot."

"Don't give me that bullshit, TJ. You were there, and whether you saw it or not you know what happened. Now talk to me, and maybe I can keep these two cops away from you. Now what happened?"

"First, you can't go to them and get them off my ass. If you do that, they will start asking why, and no matter what you tell them they won't believe you and you'll put us both at risk," I told her.

She sat there for a full two minutes without speaking. "Okay, but tell me anyway."

I told her the whole story. "So don't worry about the two cops; I will figure out how to deal with them. One thing you can do though. Casper is around somewhere, and if Kenny finds him, one of them won't be around much longer."

She was writing in her notebook. "What is his real name?"

I had to think about that one. At first I wasn't even sure I knew his name. "William Carr. The last I heard he was living at some apartments behind Ray High School."

"Where are you going to be?" she asked.

"I don't know yet. I am going to start out going north I think. Other than that I can't tell you. I just need to get away for a few days. When I get somewhere I will call Sherry, check with her in a couple of days," I explained.

"When are you leaving?" she asked.

"As soon as I pay my bill," I told her.

She reached across the table and took my hand. "Be careful, TJ, we need you and I have gotten kind of used to the idea of you being around."

"I will be fine. Like I said, I just need some down time. I never expected the pressure to come on so heavy and so quickly. I need to reevaluate this whole thing and decide how I am going to get on with it," I told her.

"I understand that. From my side this is pretty cut and dry; find out who is making the stuff, shut them down and send them to jail. With you there are greater dynamics working here. These are people who were or are very important in your life."

"It isn't so much about the guys who are involved with making and selling the meth. I just don't want to see others get hurt," I explained.

"Then we see it the same," she said. "Where is the problem?"

"I know there are some who are aware of what is happening, and in your world they go down too. In my world they are brothers, and I have to find a way to protect them."

She sat there for a minute. "TJ, I will help you protect anyone who is not directly involved, but you have to keep me in the loop. You have to trust me."

I sat there looking at the table then up to her. "It goes against the grain for me to trust you that much. You're gonna have to give me some time to mull this over. I'm not sure where I'm headed but I need to get away from here for a couple of days and work through this without anyone in my ear."

"Okay, TJ, you have my numbers if you need to talk to me. I will touch base with Sherry and tell her you had to run out of town for a couple of days. I will be waiting for your call," she said as she walked out of the bar.

I paid the bill and headed north. The big bike rumbled under me and I could feel the tension blowing off me with each mile. By the time I passed through Sinton, I felt like a new man. Out on the road again, I turned the bike around and headed back to Aransas Pass then to Port Aransas. Once there I headed for the beach, stopped at a little bait shop and picked up some beer, a couple of sandwiches, chips and a large beach towel then headed down the beach.

I found a place that was lit only by the moon and stars then pulled up the bike and kicked the stand down on a chunk of wood. The sandwiches were gone in a matter of minutes, as was the first beer. I popped the second one and just lay back on the towel and closed my eyes. I didn't realize I had fallen asleep until I heard a female voice.

"Excuse me, can you help me," came the question from a woman I could hardly see.

"Well, I don't know whether I can or not. What seems to be the problem?"

I still couldn't see her face but her voice seemed young. "I stupidly slipped off the hard pack and into soft sand. I tried a couple of times to get it out but I realized I wasn't going anywhere and didn't want to bury it completely."

I got up. "Okay, no promises but let's take a look. Where is it?"

"Just down the beach a hundred yards or so," she said.

We walked down the beach until we got to her red 1965 Mustang fastback, which was buried to the axel. "I'm glad you stopped trying to get out," I said, noting marks in the sand where the door had opened.

The moon shone off her dark hair. "I guess I tried a little too hard."

"Okay, get on the other side and start pulling sand from under the car. We have to get it back on solid ground."

The sun was just coming up when we finally got the Mustang chassis clear of the sand. Now with the sun up I could see she had nosed into a log causing the car to bury itself. I dislodged the log, pulled it back and saw it was actually closer to hard packed sand by going forward. I cleared sand from in front of both front and rear wheels so that I might have a running start.

"Okay, I will either make it out or bury it deeper. Stand back," I told her.

I started the car and was pleased to hear the rumble of the small block V-8. Though I am not a great fan of automatic transmissions, I was glad for it when I started rocking the car back and forth. The little Mustang rocked back until I felt the tires slip a bit then I slammed it in low and took it forward. After three or four times of rocking back and forth, the car began creeping forward. I felt the tires slip again and slowly pushed the accelerator down then jammed it to the floor throwing a rooster tail of sand out the back of the car. The car dropped into the sand until it found traction and scooted forward. Once on hard packed sand, I rolled the car back toward the water, pulled up next to her, and got out of the car.

She was covered with sand from head to toe. "What happened?" I asked.

"When you hit the gas I was standing behind the car," she said.

I tried hard to keep from laughing but air slipped through my lips. "I'm sorry," I said fighting back the laugh. "Come on, let's go down to the water and get this sand off you. By the way, I'm TJ, TJ Hamlin."

"I'm Sandy," she said.

"You certainly are," I replied.

"No, my name is Sandra, my friends call me Sandy," she told me.

I completely lost it. I couldn't stop laughing. "I'm sorry, Sandy," then broke down again.

When I finally got control of myself, I went back to the car and pulled her towel out. "Come on, let's get that sand off you. Take that dress off," I said and handed her the towel. I took her dress and began shaking the sand out of it while she washed the sand off her body. When she had rinsed off the sand and I had shaken as much sand from her sundress as I could, I held the towel while she pulled her dress back on.

She held out her hand. "Thank you. I don't know how to thank you."

I took her hand. For the first time I was able to get a good look at her. She was a touch over five feet tall, dark brown hair and the loveliest green eyes I have ever seen. She was attractive, not beautiful, but nice looking; she was slightly built, small breasts and a waist I could almost reach around with my hands. I took her hand. "You're welcome. If you really want to thank me, you could join me for breakfast."

Still holding my hand she looked at me. "I have to get the rest of the sand off my body. It is very uncomfortable, and I haven't had any sleep. Maybe a rain check," she said as she got into her car. As she drove away I realized I didn't have her phone number. Oh well, so much for the nice guy.

I walked back to the bike, wrapped up my stuff in the towel and headed back up the beach in search of a shower. There was a pier and a bathhouse back near the bait stand so I stopped at the bait stand and grabbed a bathing suit, some soap and a tent. The shower was cold but I was able to stand it long enough to get the sand out of my hair and out of those sensitive areas. I washed out my clothes—at least the sand would be gone. I went back up to a beach café and got something to eat then back up the beach to where I had been. I set up the shelter, making the legs short so as the day passed the sun would stay off me. Throwing down my towel I lay back down and was asleep in short order.

I managed to sleep until late afternoon and awoke to the sound of kids playing; my private place was now populated. I crawled out from under the shelter and looked at the people invading my space. There was a husband, wife and three children; I also noted the Buick sported Pennsylvania plates.

The man, a big burly sort, walked over. "Nice bike," he said. "I'm Howard." He looked over next to the bike and saw the hot beer sitting there. "Hey, I have some cold ones in the chest."

Suddenly I was very thirsty. "I'll trade you for a couple of cold ones," I told him.

He went to the chest and brought out an ice cold Lone Star, not my favorite but right then it was wonderful. I thanked him and knocked down half the beer and accepted an invitation to come over and sit with him. I sat down in the beach chair and he introduced me to his wife, Helen. We sat there and shot the breeze, then a while later they loaded up and headed back to their hotel.

I went out for a swim; after an hour of the surf I went back to my towel and fell asleep again. I must have been tired because it was dark when I was awakened again by a female voice. "Can you help me?"

I looked up and barely recognized Sandy. "Surely you didn't do it again," I answered.

"Nope, but I do have a heavy basket of food, and I need help eating it. I also have cold beer and wine. I told you I would give you a rain check," she replied.

My stomach grumbled. "Well, I guess we will be even. You have just saved a starving man from chewing his fingers off." I got up, went to her car and pulled out a basket and a cooler and set them under the shelter while she pulled a large blanket from the back seat.

The fried chicken certainly hit the spot, as did the beer. "Sorry, I'm not much on wine," I told her.

She smiled over her glass. "I'm not either. I tend to get a little crazy when I drink wine."

I reached over and pulled the bottle from the ice chest. "Here, let me pour some more."

CHAPTER SEVEN

I don't know what time we dozed off, but I awoke to the sound of the surf and was cold. I ran my hands across my chest and realized I had fallen asleep naked. I looked toward Sandy just as a cloud passed away from a full moon. She was naked as well, curled into a ball. I found my clothes and got dressed, then noticed the sky was starting to lighten slightly. I lay back down and woke Sandy. She wrapped her arms around me and pulled me to her. "Why are you dressed and I am laying here completely undressed?" she asked.

I looked at her lithe body. "Because I was freezing. Besides, the sun will begin coming over the horizon in a few minutes, and in fifteen minutes it will be bright as daylight."

She smiled at me. "Okay, I'll get dressed, but I would much rather snuggle with you," she said as she allowed me to get up and began pulling on her clothes.

She was almost blushing, but I couldn't help looking at her as she dressed. "You are one pretty lady."

She looked at me seriously for a moment. "TJ, I need to tell you something before we go any further, if we go any further."

"Why so serious? You aren't going to tell me you really aren't a woman, are you, because I know better than that," I laughed.

"TJ," she said quietly, "the other night when I got my car stuck, I did that on purpose to meet you."

I laughed. "Wow, you just drove by, saw me and thought I looked so great you just buried your car in the sand?"

"Not exactly," she said. "I saw you at the Blue Note the other night and stayed around until you left then followed you home. When you left the next day, I was there and followed you."

Now I was concerned. "Okay, and what did you see?"

She looked down. "I am a reporter with *The Corpus Christi Caller Times*, and I recognized Jean Marie. After you left I followed you out here. You almost lost me when you turned around and came back to Port Aransas."

I sat there for a moment then looked at her lovely face. I didn't know whether to kiss her or hit her. "You're a reporter? You followed me and know I met with a cop. What the hell are you doing? What do you want with me?"

A tear rolled down her cheek. "Nothing, TJ, I just want to be with you. When I'm with you, I am Sandy the woman, not Sandra D. Armon the reporter. I don't know why I want to be with you, but I can't help it. I do."

I looked at her beautiful eyes. "Sandy, you have no idea what you have stepped into, and the smartest thing you can do is walk away."

She began crying in earnest. "I don't want to walk away, please don't make me."

I was torn. I didn't want to go away from her, I didn't want her to go away, but I knew it was the right thing to do. "Sandy, if you knew what you stepped in to, you wouldn't feel that way."

She looked me in the eye. "Try me!"

I thought for a long time. "Okay, you say that now. Let's see what you have to say in a few minutes, but you have to promise to never say a word about this."

"I promise," she replied.

I sat there and told her about my involvement with the club and that they were involved in some things that were less than legal. I looked at her. "I am going to get on my bike and ride up the island a ways. If you aren't here when I get back, I will know the answer."

I got up, started the bike and cruised up the island a few miles then back again.

When I got back to the shelter my heart sank— her car was gone. *To hell with it, I'll just get back and do what has to be done*, I thought. I wrapped up my stuff, loaded the bike and headed for home.

On the way back I stopped and picked up a bottle of Jack Daniels Black Label. I got to the house and rolled the bike into the garage then unloaded it. I never have been one to start drinking at noon but right then I just wanted to get numb. After my second double shot I fell asleep and didn't wake until the phone rang. "I didn't do it and I sure as hell don't want to," I said into the phone.

"TJ, this is Sherry. I know this isn't really your job, but I have some guys coming in here for a birthday party tonight and I really need security tonight," she said.

I groaned, taking stock of myself then looked at the clock. It was a little after seven. "Okay, I will get there by 8:30. Give me a chance to get straight."

"I'm sorry, TJ, maybe I can call someone else.

I'm sorry I bothered you." I could hear the hurt in her voice.

"No, Sherry, I will be there. I just need to get myself squared away. I'm sorry, I didn't have a great morning and I knocked back a few but I am okay. I'll be there as soon as I can."

I could hear the relief in her voice. "Okay, thank you, TJ. I'll see you in a bit."

"I'll be there as soon as I can," I told her.

I got up and went to the bathroom to shave, shower and get some clothes on. The shower took longer than usual because I kept finding sand in every nook, crook and cranny, but it felt good to get the salt and sand off my body.

I opened the garage door and started to grab the bike then realized the street was wet and rain was falling. I moved the bike up so I could get the GTO out then fired up the car. It rumbled to life, the big block V-8 smooth and strong. I looked up to see my two police buddies pulling in behind me, not even trying to conceal the fact they were following me.

When I pulled into the parking lot of the Blue Note, they pulled in right behind me. I got out and walked back to them. "Thanks for the escort but I think I'm safe in this city."

Sergeant Dawson looked at me. "I don't know who you know or how you know them but we have been informed that you are strictly hands off."

"Well, I guess being a good boy pays off. If I am hands off what the hell are you doing here?"

"We're here because I think you're just another scumbag biker. I just want you to know I will make it my mission to take you down personally when the time comes," he said as he put the Ford in gear and backed out of the lot then squealed the tires as he ripped off down the road. I locked up the Pontiac and headed for the door.

I walked into the bar and headed for Sherry's office. She was sitting at her desk when I knocked on the door and walked in. "Thank you, TJ. They will start getting here in about an hour. How about something to eat?"

"That sounds good. I haven't had much today. Do you think they can rustle up a hamburger in the kitchen?" I asked.

I sat there thinking about what a lousy day it had turned into and decided I might as well just face the fact that I had a job to do and focus on that.

I heard noise coming from the bar. Sherry was in what appeared to be a heated discussion with a gruff looking man. I walked up beside her just in time to hear her say, "I told you, you can't come back in here. You have had to be told too many times to keep your hands off the girls, and the last time I told you, you threatened me."

The man was large with fists the size of hams. "Look bitch, if you"—

I stepped between the two of them, interrupting him. "That is not the way ladies are addressed here. It is time for you to leave."

He looked at me. God, this man was big. "I don't know who you are but you are stepping into something you know nothing about."

"I am the person who has the responsibility to make sure the ladies are protected, the furniture stays in one piece and the customers remain safe," I explained.

He shoved my chest forcing me back against Sherry. "So I guess you are going to make me behave like a good little boy?" he asked, laughing.

"I don't have any choice. You see that's my job, and if I can't do my job Sherry will fire me."

He laughed. "Tell me how it feels to be unemployed," he said as he threw a roundhouse intended to take my head off. I managed to back away and caused him to miss. Something jabbed me in the back, and I reached back to brush it away but someone pushed something into my right hand; it was a sap.

"Look, I really don't want to see anyone hurt, but I have no choice and I know I'm going to have to hurt you bad," I said, maintaining as safe a distance as possible

He continued laughing. "Please, don't worry about hurting me. Come on, kick my ass."

I was certainly glad I was able to keep someone smiling. "Just leave. You aren't welcome. Why would you want to be someplace you aren't wanted?" A part of me was so pissed at how the day turned out that I wanted to tear into him. Another part of me, the part with a brain, wanted me to head for the door and keep my 160 pounds in one piece.

He looked down. "You're right, I guess I should just leave," he said then charged me.

I managed to step aside a little but not before he caught me with a glancing blow, knocking me to the ground. I hit hard but scrambled to my feet as he got up from the floor. Damn, for someone who weighed close to two-fifty this guy could move.

"Back off," I told him, gripping the spring-loaded sap. "This is the last time I'm telling you. Leave now or I promise you, I am going to hurt you, and I am going to hurt you bad."

He wasn't laughing now as he walked toward me. "No, I'm not backing off. I am about to rip you apart. Enjoy your hospital rest," then he drove his fist into my left side.

All the air threatened to leave my body as I brought the sap down as hard as I could on the side of his head. He screamed and connected with a hard left to the side of my head. My vision blurred. I knew I had to back off and get some space between the two of us.

Before he could strike again I dropped to the floor and rolled away then got to my feet in time to see him running at me. Just as he reached me I dropped and drove my elbow up between his legs. His momentum caused him to trip over me and I stood, flipping him to the ground. I immediately dropped and slammed my elbow into his gut, knocking all the wind from him. I slammed him in the face with two hard blows and then, thinking he was out, got off the floor. As he tried to sit up I dropped behind him and wrapped my forearm around his throat, braced my hand with my right arm and began applying the choke. In a matter of seconds he blacked out.

I stood up and allowed him to drop to the floor. My ribs hurt like pure hell and my head was throbbing. His friends managed to get him to his feet, and they headed for the door. I went into Sherry's office and lay down.

Sherry walked in and sat in the chair next to the couch. She put an ice-filled cloth to the side of my head. "How bad are you hurting?"

"Hurts like hell when I try to breathe and my head feels like it is a balloon on the verge of popping," I told her.

She lifted the cloth and looked at the side of my head. "I think you need to go to the emergency room. Your face is turning purple," then she pulled open my shirt, "and your side looks worse."

"I just want to lay here for a while. Let me know when the party gets here. I'll be okay," I said, closing my eyes.

I was more than a little surprised when I woke with someone blinding me with a light. I reached up and pushed the hand away. "What the hell are you doing?" Then I realized I wasn't in Sherry's office any more. "Where am I? What is going on?"

The white coat spoke. "You are in the emergency room. I'm Dr. Hayes. It appears you have a mild concussion, and from a brief examination I would say you also have a couple of broken ribs."

"Okay, I'm fine now," I said as I sat up, realizing I didn't have any clothes on, just that stupid robe. "Where are my clothes?"

"In the first place, Mr. Hamlin, you are in no condition to do anything but lay here, and secondly I would very much like to keep you here at least overnight," said Dr. Hayes. "Before you object, I don't know whether there are further injuries and I would hate to have you go home and bleed to death."

"So you would rather have me bleed to death here," I said trying to laugh and going into spasms of pain.

"Absolutely," he said smiling. "It is a shorter drive to the morgue."

The pain in my ribs was bad but the explosions in my head were worse. "Does that mean if I stay here you can give me something for the pain?" I asked.

"We can give you something for your pain, Mr. Hamlin, but we will be waking you periodically so no complaints."

"Okay, fine, just stop the pain," I told him.

"I will go get some oxycodone. Is it okay with

you if your friends come in for a minute? I can't allow them to stay for long. Then we will get you up to a room."

"Sure, send in the clowns," I said.

Sherry was the first through the door. "Clowns? You know, if the doctor wasn't here I would see how ticklish you are."

I fought back a laugh. "Okay, I will behave if you will."

"There is someone else here to see you," she said as she opened the curtain and waved someone in. The giant who beat the crap out of me walked in, his head bowed.

"I'm sorry," he said. "I never meant to hurt you like this. I'll take care of your medical and anything else you need."

I looked at this guy in the light. I had greatly underestimated his size—he was huge, beyond huge. "I'll be okay, but you owe me a steak dinner."

"Anything, man, anything," he said.

"How did you find out I was here?" I asked.

"We were still in the parking lot when the ambulance came. I saw them take you out, and I had to make sure you were okay," he replied.

"So, do you always beat the crap out of someone then find them so you can make sure they aren't mobile?" I asked.

"I mean it, man, I am really sorry. I will do anything I can to make it right. I will stand here and let you beat the hell out of me if that helps," he answered.

"That's a pretty safe bet right now, but when I heal I may just take you up on that," I told him, knowing I would never do it.

The doctor came in. "Okay, everyone out. We are

well past visiting hours and I need to get Mr. Hamlin to a room and get him settled."

Sherry kissed me on the cheek and the big guy shook my hand and apologized again.

I called to Sherry as she was walking out. "Is that guy for real?"

"Take your shot first, and if the doctor will give me a few minutes I will explain," Sherry said.

The doctor nodded then injected something into my hip and before they could get me up to a room I blinked out. I remember them waking me and asking me questions to make sure the concussion had not caused greater damage. By the time I woke on my own it was well into the morning and someone was sitting in a chair between me and the window so I couldn't tell who it was.

"Good morning," Sherry said, "feeling any better?"

I took a few seconds to take inventory. "My head is throbbing, though not as much, and my ribs still hurt every time I move. I guess I am going to live; it hurts so much I know I'm going to live. What are you doing here so early?"

"I stayed the night. I couldn't leave my prize employee in the hands of strangers," she told me.

"What is that moose's name?" I asked. "What does that bum do for a living, beat up bulls?"

"First, he's not a bum; he's a rig manager for Fabian Oil and his name is Roger Morris. That's one good ole boy with a bucket of cash and no one to spend it on."

"You have to be kidding. He must bend the steel to build the damn rigs."

"He probably could," she said, looking away from me.

I watched her for a minute. "What's wrong, did the doctor tell you something he hasn't told me?" I asked.

There was something like shock on her face, "No, nothing like that; it's just that your bruises are showing up clearer than they did last night."

"How bad is it? Let me see, hand me a mirror."

"TJ, you don't"—she started.

I interrupted her. "What I don't want is to lay here and not know how bad I look. Give me a damned mirror."

She finally found a mirror and handed it to me. The whole side of my face was a sickening black, purple, red and yellow. I pulled down the sheet and looked at my ribs, same story there.

There was a noise at the door, and I looked up to see the doctor standing there. "Yes, Mr. Hamlin, it is as bad as it looks."

CHAPTER EIGHT

I lay there as the doctor looked me over. "Mr. Hamlin, I know this isn't your favorite place but I really don't want to allow you to go home. Before you object, I promise that if everything looks good tomorrow morning, I will let you go."

There wasn't much I could do: my head was throbbing and breathing was not a lot of fun. Two fights in one twenty-four-hour period had taken a lot out of me. "Fine, but if I am going to lay here, the least you can do is stop the damned pain."

"That much I can do. I'll send the nurse in with your shot in a few minutes. Right now you have a visitor, and I would prefer to wait until he is gone," he said as he walked toward the door.

He opened the door and Eddie came walking through. "Damn, bro, one fight is plenty for one day, don't you think?"

"Yeah, I have to remember that and pace myself a little better," I told him.

He sat down in the chair, opened the drawer of the table next to my bed and pushed a bag inside. "That might help. Look, I know we were going to talk, but that can wait until you get out of here and start feeling better."

"No, Eddie, I need to know what the hell is going on," I retorted. "The club has changed; kids are being patched. We have always had solid rules about our membership, and now it looks like someone threw the door open and every piece of shit off the street crawled through."

He sat thinking for a moment. "I guess I'm at fault there. I wanted the club to grow and Casper seemed to be doing a decent job recruiting people so I guess I turned a blind eye."

"Eddie, I want the membership records. I want to review every member in the club, and I want face time with each of them. We brought this club up five years ago, and we have held to our bylaws all along, until now. This can't go on."

"Okay, TJ, we'll sit down whenever you're ready and go through the records," he said as he was rising.

"No, Eddie, bring me the records today, or send them over. I don't have a lot more to do than sit around, so it's a prime time to do this," I told him.

"Come on, TJ, let this go."

"I think there is something you're forgetting. Since Jason and Carl left the club, I am the senior member. Don't cause me to make a war out of this," I told him sternly.

"You don't want to do that, TJ. I still hold the hammer in the club and I can rally as many guys as I need to hold my slot. Now, I'll get you the damned records but don't try threatening me," he said as he turned and left the room.

The nurse came in almost immediately and told me to bare my butt, which I did willingly.

"Such a nice backside, it's almost a shame to mar it with a needle," she said as she plunged the needle into me. Five minutes later I was in dreamland.

I don't know how long I slept, but when I woke up, I was looking through a haze at the men in the chairs next to the bed: my two favorite cops.

"Hey, Sleeping Beauty, welcome to the world of the living."

"Holy shit, I have died and gone to hell. I see Satan's henchmen are here already," I said.

Sergeant Dawson smiled at me. "Funny man. Why is it that lately every time I turn around they send me to look at your ugly puss?"

I looked back at the fat piece of shit. "So, did you guys turn in your badges and go to work for OSHA now, investigating barroom accidents?"

"The word we got was that you got into it with someone in the bar and they took you down," Kellum said.

"Well, you need to find better information. I slipped on some spilled beer," I told him.

Fat Boy looked at me. "You fell on both sides of your face?"

"Yeah, I must be clumsy. Maybe I should have become a cop. Now, get the hell out of here and let me go back to sleep. These bad dreams aren't good for my head," I said as I painfully rolled away from them.

It seemed like I had just gone to sleep again when I heard someone else come into the room. I managed to roll over to see Roger standing there.

I looked at the big man. "Damn, most people have the good fortune to wake up with some sweet angel watching over him. I wake up to find King Kong licking his chops and drinking my booze," I said noticing the glass.

He smiled. "You know, for a sick ass biker you have good taste in whiskey," he said finishing the glass then reaching for something. "Some guy stopped by and dropped this off," he said as he handed me a book with the club patch on the front.

I took the ledger and began flipping through it, but the drugs still had me blurry. "Just lay it over there for the time being. I can't concentrate on it now."

He stood up as Sherry walked in. She looked at me. "TJ, Roger and I have been talking. The doctor said you are getting out of here tomorrow, and I don't think you need to be alone yet. Roger offered his place and he will have a nurse there with you."

I thought for a minute. "Only if she promises to wear a sexy nurse outfit."

Roger laughed. "Okay, man, but I don't know if we can find one to fit a nurse weighing two-thirty."

I started laughing, and it felt like someone was kicking me in the side again. "You asshole," I said, fighting against the pain.

Sherry stood there. "Okay you two, behave or I will kick both your asses. We are going to leave now, but we'll be back in the morning to pick you up. In the meantime, rest. The nurse is on her way to make sure you sleep well."

"Oh my God, if she's Roger's nurse don't leave me here alone," I said and spasms hit my side again at my own joke.

The nurse came in and once again I drifted off.

It was dark in the room when my eyes opened to see someone in the chair again. "Who's there?" I asked.

"Jean Marie," she replied.

I started to panic. "What are you doing here? Anyone could come walking through that door. Are you really trying to get me killed?"

"Calm down, TJ, you taught me better than that. It's three in the morning, and no one knows I'm here. I just needed to check on you."

"Oh, I'm just peachy, couldn't be better," I told her.

"Glad to hear it, but I thought your head was harder than that," she jibed. "I got the whole story from Sherry. She was the one who called me. So, where are you going when you get out of here?"

"A new friend, the guy who put me here, is putting me up for a few days," I told her.

"You have the strangest way of making friends; most people run around with school chums, football team members, things like that, and when they meet new people they exchange handshakes, not fists," she laughed.

"Yeah, well, most people I run with don't talk to cops as often as I do without wearing handcuffs."

She laughed again. "Well, if it would make you feel any better I can hook you up."

I eyed her. "Don't go getting kinky on me. I might think there is a human being hiding inside that cop skin you wear."

"Okay. You need to get back to sleep, but I came here to pass along some information. I very quietly did some digging into Kenny. Everything I saw tells me Kenny is clean except for purchasing meth," she told me.

"Shauna is hooked on the stuff. He's been buying for her. Think about it, if he is buying from someone else then he must not be selling," I explained.

She thought for a moment. "That makes sense. Okay, I will see if I can get the cops off him."

"Please do. I need help from the inside, and from the looks of things he is the only one I can trust."

"Okay, but you have to promise me you will stay off the streets until you heal."

I looked at her. "You know, if my nurse looked

more like you it would be a pleasure."

"Be careful," she smiled. "You're starting to sound like some kind of human being. Okay, I am out of here. Touch base with me so I don't have to chase your ass down. Catching you right now would be way too easy," she said as the door closed.

I reached into the drawer, pulled out the bottle and took a long hit on the scotch. I lay back down and started thinking about my next step and started taking inventory of my situation. I was confident that I could trust Jean Marie and Sherry; since Roger had nothing to do with the club I was certain at very least he would not work against me. I couldn't say for sure about Kenny; his involvement with Shauna could make him an easy target. Dave was a good friend I could trust with my life, but I didn't want him in the middle of this thing; he really had no dog in this hunt. In the neutral was Eddie; there was no direct evidence that he was involved but how could he be president of the club and not have a clue about what was going on? Casper was a definite problem; he at very least wanted to kick my ass. Not much I could build a team on, not much I could call on for help.

Somewhere along the line I fell asleep, and any idea I had after that was completely lost.

It was way too early when the nurse came in and started getting me ready to get out of this place. The doctor came in and started giving me my do's and don'ts. "Mr. Hamlin, I'm still not crazy about turning you loose, but you should be fine if you follow some simple instructions." He handed me a large bottle of pills. "Your ribs are going to give you fits for a few more days. Don't overdo the pain pills and stay away from alcohol while you are taking them. Rest, and more rest; ribs will heal on their own but they will take time; don't strain. And I would strongly suggest you stay away from fights." He handed me a small card. "My phone numbers are listed there. If I'm not in the office leave a message unless it's an emergency, then call the second number—they will contact me. If it's late, the last number is my home. Use that as a last resort or a serious emergency."

Sherry and Roger came through the door. "I am beginning to think there is something going on between you two," I said. "I never see you apart anymore."

Sherry looked at Roger. "There could be worse things," she said smiling. She looked back at me. "Of course we could leave you here to find your own way out."

"Please don't do that," I said in my best whimpering voice. "They torture me here, feed me poison and stick me with all kinds of things."

"Poor little TJ," she said. "Come on, Roger has a place you can stay and we've made arrangements to have someone with you all day. After we get you settled I'll go by your place and pick up whatever you need. Then I have to get back to the bar."

I certainly was glad Roger had a big Oldsmobile, but even in it I could feel the bumps shocking my ribs. Roger's home was a huge place in a new section off Padre Island Drive. I had seen these places when they were being built and never expected to see one up close, let alone see the inside of one. I looked at Roger in the front seat. "Damn, do you own Corpus, too?"

Roger laughed. "Nah, it's too small; I'm looking at Dallas. There's a small apartment around back; you'll have plenty of privacy, and my comings and goings won't bother you."

We drove around behind the house. The "small apartment" looked anything but small. "Damn good thing I didn't need space to stretch my legs. Roger, someone said you had a little money; they didn't say it was anything like this."

Roger smiled. "I just got lucky. I was in the right place at the right time."

We pulled in front of the apartment, and I noticed there was a pool between the apartment and the main house. Sherry and Roger helped me out of the car and into the apartment. The door led into a small entry then into a large living room fully equipped with a large television, a tremendous stereo and a collection of records that looked larger than my local music store. The furniture was all leather and the room was decorated like an old ranch house. There were two bedrooms, the largest of which was about the size of my apartment. The kitchen was made for a chef. I made my way to the leather recliner and found it was a bit painful to lean the chair back, but once there I was in heaven.

Sherry came over and kissed me on the cheek. "I have to get to the bar and get ready for tonight. You just relax and finish getting well." Then she walked out the door.

Roger sat down on the couch. "TJ, I want to talk to you about something. I spend a good part of the year out on the rigs and I have to pay a company to keep an eye on this place. I would appreciate it if you would consider just moving in here, rent free. All you have to do is look out for my property while you're here."

I sat there and thought about it. "That's a generous offer but you don't know anything about me and you should be well aware of who is in your house."

The smile on his face hid something. "Maybe I know all I need to know."

"No matter what you think you know, you don't know enough," I told him.

The smile grew even larger. "Well, how about if I start with you getting booted out of the Navy. I know that is a lie. The Navy asked you to look into something involving your old club. Jean Marie is your contact and you don't know what to think of her. This part I don't know for sure but my guess is that what you're doing has something to do with drugs."

"Who the hell have you been talking to?" I demanded. "The information you have could get me killed. If you know this much, who else knows?"

His smile grew even larger. "Actually, the only part I knew for sure was the Navy, and I suspected Jean Marie. The rest of it was just what I suspected. TJ, I know I don't look like I have enough brains to walk and chew gum at the same time, but I'm not a stupid man. I started out as a dirty-assed roughneck and paid attention to what the next guy up was doing and I moved, step by step. Now, I'm sitting on top of a huge salary and a roll in the bank that would choke a horse."

"I understand that, and I don't think you are stupid, but if you can figure out this stuff, someone else can as well," I said.

"TJ, you have to trust someone. You can't Lone Ranger this thing. You better figure this thing out while you're on your ass. I have to fly out to one of the rigs, but I'll be back in about a week. This place is yours if you want it no matter what you decide, and I am here for whatever you need but I'm in all the way, or leave me out. Now, give me a list of what you need and I'll make sure you get it," he said as he walked toward the door.

"I need to think this through, Roger. I don't want to be responsible for someone else getting hurt, or worse," I told him.

"Just make out your list and I'll pick it up later. Your nurses will start showing up this afternoon. Let them take care of you, do what they say and just relax," then he walked out the door.

CHAPTER NINE

Sherry

When I graduated from high school the world was a different place. It was 1960 and there was no war, unemployment was below five percent. Most people who wanted to work were working. I was dating Jerry Davis who I had been dating since we were in the eighth grade together. I was all set to go to college when the rabbit died—I was eighteen and pregnant. Back in that time the honorable thing to do was to get married and we did.

Jerry was a mechanic at a small garage making just enough money to cover expenses. Every month was a struggle, and I was constantly borrowing from my parents, always promising to pay them back but they knew better. In 1961 our daughter Andria was born and even as bad off as we were she could brighten even my darkest day. I named her after my grandmother who had died just a few weeks before Andria was born. My father was happier than I had seen him in years; he had a granddaughter and a reminder of his mother. Jerry and I continued to struggle with no expectation of things getting better. Jerry's way of dealing with it was to sit in a bar until he no longer had any cash in his pockets, leaving me and Andria to get to know one another even better. One night he came home drunk and slapped me around, busting my lip and blacking my eye. My father almost killed him the next night.

When Andria was six months old Jerry came in drunk and broke, and I got an idea. Since he was giving all his money to the bar, maybe I could find a job in a bar and get some back. I called a friend of mine from high school and asked her if she could help me. Since Jean Marie was on the police force I thought she might know a place I could look. She called me a few days later and told me about a place owned by a very nice couple. I went to work at the Blue Note and was soon making some pretty good money.

Jerry didn't like it. I was embarrassing him by working but the other choice was to stop drinking and come home every night, something he just wasn't willing to do. Mom and Dad took care of Andria at night while I worked. It was hard, but I was getting up early after working late so Andria had as normal a life as possible.

I had been working at the Blue Note about seven months when I came home after a hard shift and Jerry snatched my purse away from me pulling all my tips out. I tried to stop him but all I got for my trouble was a hard slap followed by an attack that left me bruised in a number of places. As soon as he took my money and left, I called Jean Marie and, abiding her suggestion, I decided to file charges against him. Jean Marie showed up at the house twenty minutes after I talked to her. As soon as she walked in the door she called my parents and told them to meet us at the hospital. I was unable to get off the couch so she got Andria dressed, loaded me in the car and we headed for the hospital. On the way to Spohn Hospital she put out an all-points bulletin for Jerry, indicating what he had done to me and that he was intoxicated.

I must have been worse off than I thought,

because they rushed me into the emergency room, ripped off my clothes and began examining me. Jerry was the only person who had seen me naked except my parents when I was much younger; having a bunch of strangers moving over every inch of my body embarrassed me to no end. When the doctor asked me where I hurt, I explained that my hands and feet didn't hurt; the rest was on fire with pain. I was given something that lessened the pain as the doctors finished their examination. The doctor explained I had three broken ribs, my cheek bone on the left side was shattered and would require extensive rework and my jaw was broken. On top of this was internal bleeding, but they were unsure what was bleeding; surgery was necessary and urgent.

I begged them to allow me to see my daughter and my parents before they took me into surgery. I held Andria close, her sleeping body stirring only slightly. My father saw me for the first time and he began to weep openly along with my mother. As my father kissed me on the cheek he whispered, "I am going to find that son of a bitch. He'll be dead before you wake up."

It hurt like hell to speak but I managed. "Dad, Jean Marie is already taking care of it. I'll need both you and Mom to take care of Andria until I can take care of her myself. You can't do that from the inside of a jail." I don't remember what happened after that for a few days. In fact it was over a week before I saw anything but the inside of my eyelids.

The police stopped Jerry twenty minutes after the all-points bulletin went out and arrested him for drunk driving. Once he had sobered up enough to be questioned, it was explained to him that he was also under arrest for assault as well as driving while drunk.

He was also told the assault charge could be changed to attempted murder depending on the doctor's report. Jean Marie told me they refused his request for bail and he would remain in jail until he went to court.

My parents told me Andria was doing fine but missed me and Dad had stayed in the hospital while I was in surgery instead of going after Jerry. They had also cleared out my apartment and moved everything to their house because I wouldn't be able to work for a while and couldn't cover those expenses. My parents were wonderful through the whole ordeal. My dad had never liked Jerry and had told me our marriage would not last long, but he never said "I told you so" and was right there when I needed something.

Mr. and Mrs. Stellson, the owners of the Blue Note, stopped by a few times and always brought something for me as well as Andria. They told me they had hired another girl with the understanding that when the time came my spot would be there for me. They also helped with the hospital bills and co-signed a note for the rest.

As painful as it was physically, I went to court when Jerry's case was heard. I think he was more than a little surprised when I went to the stand and testified as to how he had mistreated, abused and beat me on more than one occasion. After the prosecutor finished with me, Jerry's attorney jumped in. "How long have you been sleeping around while your husband has been working, Mrs. Davis?"

I was so angry I wanted to scream, but when the prosecutor objected I had time to calm down. The judge overruled the objection so I was forced to answer the question. I looked at Jerry and then back to his lawyer. "Unlike my husband I get up at six in the morning to get our daughter up so I can bathe and feed her. Then I fix my husband's breakfast and get him out of bed then fix his lunch. While he is at work I care for our daughter and the apartment. At five o'clock, the time he is supposed to be in from work, I begin fixing dinner. Most of the time I end up eating alone because he is sitting in a bar somewhere drinking his paycheck. Then I get ready for work and drop Andria off at my parents' house then get to work by seven. I get off at one in the morning, pick up my daughter and go home where I get about four hours sleep before I get up and start all over again."

He smirked. "I asked you about the fact that you are sleeping with another man while your husband is gone. What does all of that have to do with my question?"

"Can you tell me when I have time?" I asked. I could see the prosecutor smile and the judge snicker as the lawyer decided he had no more questions for me.

Jerry was found guilty of assault, and the judge asked if he had anything to say that might influence his verdict and punishment. Jerry stood up. "This ignorant bastard who must have failed law school wouldn't allow me to testify, so I will do that now."

The judge banged his gavel. "I will not tolerate that kind language in my courtroom. If you have something to say, do so without the use of vulgarity."

Jerry smirked. "You must not be married. You have no idea what vulgarity is until you have had to put up with some bitch nagging your ass all the time. That's why I drink; if I go home I have to listen to her whining, griping and nagging and her daughter is just like her. My wife forced me to marry her; she got pregnant on purpose just so she could sink her hooks deeper into me."

"Mr. Davis, you have said nothing thus far that would give me cause not to give you the maximum penalty under the law," the judge said.

Jerry looked shocked. "In the first place, I am not guilty. I never touched her. This is some kind of trick cooked up by her and her parents. I am a good husband, I work hard, so I have a few drinks after work to relax before I have to go home and face her."

"So, Mr. Davis, you are saying you didn't get drunk and beat your wife. That means that either your wife is intentionally misleading the court or you are being less than honest," the judge said.

"Now you understand. I never touched her, I don't know how she got hurt. Maybe she did it to herself or her boyfriend did it," Jerry said, acting as though he had just won.

"I further suspect that you deny being intoxicated," the judge queried.

"I might have had two beers when the police stopped me, Your Honor," was his reply.

"And you are being as truthful about that as you are about your statement that you didn't beat your wife," he asked.

"That's right," Jerry said proudly.

"In that case my decision will be quite simple," the judge said. Jerry's smile was wide across his face. "The blood test you agreed to indicates your blood alcohol level was point one three percent at the time of your arrest. I can only surmise you were not being truthful when you said you only had two beers. By your own statement you indicated you were being as truthful about your denial of assaulting your wife as you were about not being intoxicated; therefore, by your own words I find you guilty of assault. I can't hear the case of drunk driving, though I would love to; that case will be heard in traffic at a later date. Mrs. Davis, do you have anything to say to the court before I sentence your husband?" he asked.

Talking was so painful, but I had to be heard even with my jaw wired shut. "Your Honor, for some time I have tolerated my husband's abuse. I know I should have done something about it long ago, but I kept hoping things would get better; instead it just got worse. Now I fear for my life and I fear what my father would do if Jerry ever touched me again. I beg you to keep him in jail as long as possible," then sat down exhausted by the effort.

"Mr. Davis, are you ready to hear the decision of this court," the judge said to Jerry.

As Jerry stood, he began, "This is bullshit, you can't do this. I will app…"

The judge slammed his gavel so hard it sounded like a gunshot in the small room. "Jerry Davis, you have nothing to say that I want to hear and if you open your mouth I will add as much time as possible to your sentence. Now, for perhaps the first time in your life, shut up and take what is coming to you like a man."

The judge opened a large book on his bench. "I have looked deeply into this and I was struck that the law indicates a maximum of 180 days in jail and a ten thousand dollar fine," he said looking at Jerry who was now smiling. "However," he continued, "when there is evidence that the violence has escalated over time, a more severe sentence may be passed down. Further, the attack on Mrs. Davis took place in the presence of your child and that allows for a still greater punishment. So the following is pronounced by the court: you shall serve six years for the assault with an additional five years for the assault taking place in the presence of a child."

Jerry turned around and looked at me. "You stupid bitch, you don't know what a beating is yet. When I get out I am going to show you what real pain is!"

The judge sat there with a smile on his face. "Thank you, Mr. Davis. Your threat just added three years. You now have fourteen years to serve. Is there anything else you would like to say or have you dug a deep enough hole for yourself?" Hearing nothing, he banged his gavel proclaiming the end of the hearing.

When the bailiff had the handcuffs on Jerry, the judge called us to the bench. "Mr. Davis, I wanted Mrs. Davis to hear this off-the-record discussion. Mr. Davis, the worst of criminals take a dim view of wife beaters and child abusers. My goal is to ensure that you have the opportunity to spend some time around the meanest, nastiest scum who inhabit our prison system. Enjoy your stay," then he got up and left as the bailiff escorted Jerry from the room.

It seemed like forever before I could get back to work, but I spent that time enjoying Andria. It was heartwarming to watch my father with her. I told my parents I was going back to work in a couple of weeks. My parents decided they would like to take a couple of weeks and do some traveling before I went back to work so they could be there when it was time. I had not known my parents to take a vacation since I had left home and we no longer went together. Little did I know the bomb that was about to drop into my life.

They had been gone for nine days when I received a call from the state police. There had been an accident and both my parents were in the hospital

in New Orleans. I didn't know what to do so I called
Jean Marie who came right over and helped me sort
through the options. In the end her mother was happy
to take Andria until I could get back and Jean Marie
loaned me the money to make the trip. It would have
been much faster to fly but then I would have had to
rent a car and I didn't have the money for that so
I drove.

It was late when I hit New Orleans, and I didn't
know where the hospital was. I drove around until I
found a police officer who escorted me right to the
front door and even went in with me to make sure I
got to the right place. They wouldn't allow me to see
them and after I told them I had very limited funds
they took me to a room that was used by the nurses
and doctors where I was able to sleep for a few hours.

It was their doctor who woke me. Standing there
with him was a chaplain. I knew then it wasn't good.
The doctor explained that my father had died only a
few hours after I had been contacted and my mother
was on life support. I sat there and bawled for what
seemed like hours as the two men did what they could
to comfort me. I finally got that out of my system and
asked if I could see my mother. The doctor sat down
close to me. "Mrs. Davis, the only reason we have
kept your mother on life support was to give you the
opportunity to get here. I will take you to her but only
if you insist. The accident was a bad one, and I am
afraid your mother's injuries are very serious. This
may not be the way you want to remember your
mother."

I told him I appreciated his concern but I had to
see her. Both men went with me as we went to the
critical care unit. I stood outside the door and started
crying again. That year had been so terrible; first

dealing with all the drinking and abuse by Jerry, then the final abuse that put me in the hospital and now this. As I stood there, though, I thought about my dad and remembered how much he enjoyed doting over Andria, about how close we had all become as I recovered from my injuries. Then I began to cry once more as I realized what Andria would miss with my parents being gone. I finally went into the room. I didn't recognize her as my mother; she was so swollen and bruised that her features were completely distorted. I had been with her a little over an hour when the doctor came in. "It's time, Mrs. Davis."

I knew I had to let her go. It really wasn't her lying in that bed. I looked at the doctor again. "My father, may I see him now?"

"Mrs. Davis, I must very strongly suggest you don't do this. Your father was hurt much worse than your mother; he was in a lot worse condition," he responded.

"Doctor, in the last year I have faced some issues that I would never have been able to tolerate if not for them. I need to see him," I said suddenly.

The doctor shrugged his shoulders and took me to the lower parts of the hospital. We stood outside a room marked "Morgue."

"Once again," the doctor pleaded, "please don't go in there. There is nothing in there for you." Seeing my resolve he opened the door and we walked to the very back of the cold room.

As I stood in front of the table he stepped back slightly. I stood there for a moment then with shaking hands I began pulling back the sheet covering his body. My legs were shaking and as I looked down I felt my world tilt and myself falling. I knew I was falling but I couldn't stop myself, then the room spun into darkness. When I came to I was in an office lying on a couch. I began to sit up, feeling the room spin a bit.

"Just lay there for a few more minutes," the doctor told me. "I managed to break your fall but you still hit pretty hard."

The shock was amazing, I thought I could deal with anything but I was proven wrong. I spent the next hour signing papers, making arrangements for their release, not knowing how I was going to pay for it. They tried to talk me into waiting until the next day to leave but I had a great need to get out of there and get back to my daughter. The drive back seemed to take forever and when I arrived home I was tired and it was late but I wanted to be with Andria—without her I was completely alone.

The next few days were a blur. I was moving on automatic pilot, without much thought. I was able to borrow enough money to get my parents home and to cover the funeral. Now I was broke and in debt; this was not a very good year at all. I was sitting in the dark dreariness of my parents' living room when someone knocked on the door. I had been ignoring people's knocks all day, but I answered this time for some reason. An older gray haired man in an expensive suit was standing at the door with his hat in his hands. He looked familiar but I didn't know why.

He expressed his sorrow at my parent's passing then introduced himself as the attorney who was assigned as executor to my parents' estate. In the next thirty minutes I discovered my parents had left all there was for me and a nice fund for Andria. The sum of what they left me made my head spin, the most surprising of which was a 1958 Thunderbird my father had rebuilt from the ground up.

★ ★ ★

I pretended to sleep as Sherry told me her story, liking the way her voice sounded in the darkness of Roger's guesthouse; the nurse had left hours ago.

"To make a long boring story short," she went on, "I eventually bought the Blue Note and remodeled my parents' home, making it my own. That pretty much brought me to the day that Jean Marie came to my office to ask a favor; of course I told her I would do whatever she needed. That was when she told me about this guy named TJ and the whole situation and asked me to hire him, also informing me that whatever I paid him would be reimbursed.

"I hadn't expected to like you, TJ, but I found you to be a wonderful combination of good looks along with a toughness and tenderness you don't often see in a man. I immediately liked you, and if you were just a few years older I could provide you a warm place to sleep at night—then again, age is but a number."

I smiled inside and kept my eyes closed.

"So, there you have it," she finished. "That's how I became involved with a man who brought more living back into my life than I ever thought existed for me."

CHAPTER TEN

After a week of lying around being pampered and basically treated like an invalid, I was about ten minutes away from going stir crazy. I had gone through the entire membership and found a number of people I had my doubts about, and now I was bored. I popped two more pills and washed them down with Dalwhinnic fifteen-year-old single malt then lay back preparing to doze off when the ringing of the door bell shook me into reality. My night nurse answered the door and was arguing with someone quietly at first then shouting.

Jean Marie stormed into the room. "Will you tell the white hat Gestapo I am not a home invader?"

I broke into a laugh. "You better tell her. I don't speak Spanish and she doesn't speak English."

Jean Marie turned to the woman rattling off something in Spanish. I managed to catch a couple of words that aren't used in polite conversation. The nurse looked at me with pleading eyes. I waved her off telling her it was okay.

I was feeling no pain from the pills and scotch and something about the whole thing struck me as so funny I couldn't stop laughing. When I finally stopped, I looked at her. "Okay, you come barging into my home, upset my nurse and interrupt a perfectly good drunk; there has to be more reason than to look at my handsome face."

"Actually I am just here to see how you are

coming along and see when you are going to get back to work," she said.

I looked at her in mock anger. "Damn, here I am beaten half to death and all you can think about is when I am going to get back on the job. Damn, you are one cold-hearted witch."

She wasn't sure whether I was joking or not. "I'm not pushing, just wondering."

I smiled at her. "I know, I'm just kidding and I am okay. My ribs are a little tender but the headaches are gone. I'm ready to get back in the saddle. I just need to work through some things here."

She leaned toward me resting her elbows on her knees. "Like what?"

I poured another scotch and offered her one. She went to the bar and got a glass then poured herself two fingers. I took a drink. "Someone convinced me that I am taking on this whole thing by myself and I'm being foolish. I need to figure out who I can trust and who I want involved. What did you find out about Kenny and have you gotten people off his ass?"

She took a long drink. "First, as I said before, Kenny is clean except for making buys of meth and pot. I don't think he would make a good witness, but I am as certain as I can be he is not selling. As for him being watched, not any more; they are off him, at least for now."

"So that makes three of us. I feel like I can trust Sherry, but this might be more than she can handle," I told her.

"Sherry is a pretty tough little girl. She has been through some very hard times and came out on top. She is as rugged and trustworthy as they come. That's why I chose her place for you to work."

"Okay, so now I have three I can trust, but I have

to do some serious thinking before I include Sherry. I am afraid this thing will get nasty and people can get hurt," I said.

"Okay, so where do we go from here?" she asked

"First I'm going out tomorrow and talk to Eddie about the membership concerns I have. I really believe a part of the answer is right there. Then we will see where we go from there," I explained.

We talked for a little longer, just general bullshit. She finished her drink and headed for the door. Me, I headed for bed, thinking about what the next day would bring.

In the four months since leaving the Navy, I felt I was losing my identity. Before I joined the Navy I was a biker and member of CC Riders, then the numerous definitions the Navy gave me. Now I was...what? Was I a cop, biker, Navy? I just didn't know. These thoughts and many more spun through my head as I tried unsuccessfully to fall asleep. Finally around three in the morning I dropped off.

The Sun came up a little too early even if it was almost eleven when I finally lifted my head from the pillow. As soon as I did, my ribs screamed at me and I slowly managed to get to my feet and move toward the shower by way of the kitchen to start the coffee. I turned the water as hot as I could stand it then gradually made it hotter still, and I began to feel myself loosen up a little. A couple of cups of coffee and a couple of pain pills made me feel like I might be able to face the world.

My bike had been sitting in the garage for too long to start easily. On the first kick it felt like my ribs were being punched again. It took three more before the big engine found its breath and roared to life. I eased in the choke and let the Harley idle for another minute before dropping it into first and rolling out of the garage. I popped another pain pill before heading down the street toward the highway. It felt good to get out, and I rolled the throttle when I hit Padre Island Drive and let the beast have its head. Soon the speedometer was passing ninety and I backed off a bit. A few miles later I turned the bike back and pointed in the direction of the clubhouse.

As I expected Eddie's bike was out front along with one I was certain belonged to Casper. I shut the bike down a couple of blocks from the clubhouse and glided to a spot behind the clubhouse where the bike couldn't be seen. I eased down the stand and slowly and painfully slid from the bike seat. I slipped around the building until I was right below an open window in the main room. I crept up until I could see inside, and sure enough it was Casper in the room. I couldn't hear what they were saying at first then they must have shifted because words became clearer.

"Look, Eddie, we have way too much in this business to shut it down now. Besides, we promised product, and if we don't fill the bill there will be hell to pay," I heard Casper say.

"Okay, but you got to keep the other guys out of sight. TJ is hot to trot about those guys, particularly your two little buddies. If he sees them again things are going to get rough," Eddie said.

"Why did you let that asshole have membership?"

Eddie was quiet a moment. "Look, the charter supports it and if I hadn't held up the charter he would have gone ballistic. Don't sweat it. Things will cool down and everything will be okay. Besides, TJ is going to need some cash—that bouncer gig won't satisfy him long."

"So what? You gonna cut him in on this?" asked Casper.

Eddie laughed. "Hell, no! I will eventually talk him into working at the shop and pay him enough to keep him satisfied, and I can keep an eye on him."

"Look, Eddie, I can take him out easy enough and no one will know what happened to him," Casper protested.

Eddied laughed again. "Then you better find someone else to do it. He was about to make you eat sand at Padre that day. Besides, that big guy he's been hanging with concerns me."

Now Casper was laughing. "He's just a big tub of shit. We will just get him out of the way."

I heard a hardness in Eddie's voice. "Look, you better do a lot of thinking before you even consider acting. If TJ finds out you or I had anything to do with this, he will kill us both."

"Bullshit, man, I don't see how he could know I had anything to do with it and even if he did you're covered."

"Covered by you? Look, Casper, I love you like a brother but you would tell him anything he wants to know if he got his hands on you; you would squeal like a little girl. Look, just get out of here and take care of the stuff."

"Okay, I'm outta here. I'll be at the trailer for the next couple of days with the guys so we can get this load out of the way. This should net us a few hundred thou at least," Casper said, his voice getting lower.

I heard the door close then a few minutes later the two bikes fired up and headed out. I pushed my bike around the corner and put it in front of the clubhouse. I had every right to be there so why hide it? I went to the clubhouse door and tried my old key and was only mildly surprised that it worked. I went in and headed for the office; *that* lock had been changed. I took my Buck and worked the cheap latch and soon slipped it. I quickly and carefully went through every drawer in the desk and the file cabinet, finding nothing at all. I locked the office again when I heard a motorcycle pulling into the lot. I went to the fridge and grabbed a beer, popped the top and quickly poured half of it down the drain.

Kenny came through the door. "Hey, bro, good to see you out of the pin."

I took a sip from the beer and leaned against the old pool table. "I couldn't take it any longer. I was going stir crazy. How is Shauna doing?"

He grabbed a beer and came over next to me. "She's pretty rough. Casper either doesn't have any more or he has decided to cut her off. I was about half hoping to find him here."

I sat there for a minute. "Wait here, Kenny, let me make a call and see what I can do." I went to the phone and called Jean Marie's office. She answered almost immediately. "You know who this is," I said. "Can we talk freely?"

She was silent for a few seconds. "Not really. Can we meet in a half hour?"

I looked at Kenny. "Sure, I'll be there in about twenty minutes." She hung up without saying anything else. Then I turned to Kenny. "You know where Dave's is, right?"

"The bait shop near the causeway? Yeah, I know it."

"Okay, wait ten minutes after I leave and meet me out there. Pull your bike behind the building and come in the back door," I told him.

I got to the bike and headed for Dave's. It wasn't

a long trip from the clubhouse but I wanted to get there ahead of Jean Marie. I watched to see if anyone was following. I had no reason to believe there would be anybody there, but I was growing a bit paranoid. I got to Dave's and pulled around back, parking the bike where it wouldn't easily be seen even if someone parked behind the building.

I walked in and found Dave in his usual place. "Dave, I need to talk to you and I want you to think seriously about what I am going to say."

He looked at me and noted I was rather serious. "Hey, bro, you know I am here for whatever you need."

I hated this, I hated including him, but people already knew Dave and I were friends, and if they came looking for me this was one place they would look. "Dave, I am involved in something with the police, the Navy and the club, and you deserve to know what's going on. It could get dangerous and it could get nasty."

The look on his face told me he was starting to understand. "TJ, I wouldn't have a wonderful wife and family if it wasn't for you. Whatever you need, whatever you want me to do, just say the word."

I quickly explained the whole situation to him, trying not to leave anything out. "So, what do you think?"

"Nothing changes, man. I'm here as far as you need me," he said with a tone that told me he had enough sense to be a little scared.

I heard Kenny come around behind the store. "I have a couple of people coming and we need a place to talk. Can we use your office?"

"It's yours, whatever you need. There is a buzzer in there that Maria used to use to page me from the front. If someone shows up, I'll buzz you."

"Okay, Jean Marie will be here in a few minutes. Point her in our direction if no one is in the front. Dave, I have a question that may seem a little strange. Do you know anyone who handles meth?" I asked.

He had a confused look on his face. "Sure, one of Maria's brothers. Why?"

"I can't explain, but can I touch him for a few hits?" I asked as I rolled off a hundred dollars.

"Okay, TJ, I have to trust you aren't going to bust him," he said.

"I wouldn't do that to you, Dave," I said then turned to see Kenny come through the back door. I pointed toward the office and went in with him.

I explained I had some stuff coming for Shauna then sat down. We just talked about general bullshit until the door opened and Jean Marie walked in. I introduced the two of them and explained to Kenny. I could tell right away that he was leery of the situation, "Kenny, we aren't looking to bust you or Shauna. We are after the people in the club that are doing this. They are killing people, Kenny; just look what has happened to Shauna."

Kenny was actually sweating. "TJ, they are our brothers, they are the only family I have known, and you are talking about sending them to jail, busting up the club."

"The club will survive if the right people are there, bro. Think back, man, remember the days we used to party like hell and ride until our asses were sore? Where are those days? Is the club really a club any more or just a drug business?" I asked.

He looked down at his hands, trying to take in all he had heard. Then Jean Marie spoke up. "Kenny, I don't know you, but TJ trusts you, and right now he needs people around him he can trust."

"Look man, I need some time. I can't get my head around this right now," he responded.

I looked at him and grabbed his shoulder. "That's cool, Kenny, take all you need and if the answer is no I'll understand, no hard feelings. Just don't trip on me to Eddie or Casper."

"Never, man, you know that," he said in earnest. Just then the buzzer went off and I went to the front. Dave handed me a bag, and I took it back to Kenny.

"Here, this should hold Shauna until we can figure out how to get her the help she needs," I said as I gave the bag to him. "Look, we are meeting at Roger's house at five tomorrow afternoon. If you feel like you want to be a part of this, meet us there. If you change your mind and want to split, that's cool. The only people who will be there are people I know I can trust." I stood up and gave him a hug as he left.

"Okay, I know you didn't just call me here to watch you pass drugs to your friend. What's up?" Jean Marie asked.

"No, I didn't ask you here for that and I know how uncomfortable you were, but allow me a few minutes," I said.

"A little uncomfortable?" she said, her voice rising an octave. "Just being here when you did that could cost me my job and jail time!"

I sat there quietly until she stopped her tirade. "Fine, are you through now? Listen Little Miss Clean Hands, your hands are going to come off just a little dirty before this is over, so if you are functioning under some illusion that I am the only one to get dirty in this thing, we better shut down right now."

"Look, I'm your liaison here, not a co-conspirator. You are the one under cover, you are the one who gets his hands dirty," she went on.

I stood up, walked from the room, got on the bike and tore out of the parking lot like the devil himself was on my tail. I rolled the throttle and watched the speedometer climb past a hundred as I blew through the gears. As I rolled closer to town I dropped my speed to legal limits to keep the man off my ass. I climbed over the bridge and headed for Blasters. When I got there I was the only white face in the place, but Carl came over and shook my hand and everyone's eyes moved away from me.

"So, what's up, little brother?" he said. "You have that look on your face that says you wanna rip someone's face off."

I looked in the mirror. He was right—I looked like I wanted trouble, any kind of trouble. I looked back at him. "I need a double of the best scotch you have and none of your watered down stuff."

He even showed me the bottle as he poured a long double. "So, what's up? I haven't seen you in a few weeks."

I took half the drink down. "I have myself in a mess and I am not sure what to do about it. I just need to chill and think." I threw twenty on the bar. "Mind if I hold the rest of this?" I asked.

He took the twenty, nodded, pushing the bottle to me and I headed for a dark corner. Texas law only allowed hard liquor sales at private clubs and stores, not in bars. By him "giving" me the bottle he wasn't really violating the law. I poured another drink and sat there in the dark. I noticed every eye in the house suddenly cage on the door. When I looked up, I saw Jean Marie come in and look around. It took her a minute to find me in my hiding place. "Buy a girl a drink?" she asked. I got up and went to the bar and got another glass and set it in front of her. She looked at me. "You won't even pour it for me?"

I looked back at her. "I'm afraid my hands are too dirty for that. I might contaminate your glass. Pour your own, have your say, and get the hell out of here."

She poured a drink and took a swallow. "Okay, can we start this night over? I really think we got way off track and I might not have helped the situation."

I poured myself another drink. "Do you always drink this slow?" I asked.

"You really aren't going to let up, are you? Look, TJ, this is new ground we're covering. I am as new to all this as you are and there are going to be times when I don't handle things very well. I'll say the wrong things and screw up just like everyone else. You can't understand and forgive that?" she asked.

"Here is what I understand. People make mistakes and they say they are sorry, no big deal; we'll just have a do-over. If you or I make a mistake and it causes someone to lose trust in us, we can be in very big trouble; no do-over," I told her.

"I'm just not used to dealing with people who are on the outer borders of the law. I don't handle it very well I guess," she said. Just then a rather large black man came over and leaned against her chair.

He looked at me to see if I was going to challenge him, but I just smiled. He bent down between us. "Hey baby, why don't you leave whitey here and come join me?" I saw Carl moving our way, and I waved him off.

She looked at him. "For one thing your breath smells like you have been licking a dog's butt. Secondly I am talking to whitey and I hate being interrupted. Third, if you don't leave and return to your table I will have to do something you may regret later."

I couldn't see his face but I knew he was smiling. Big mistake. "Look little girl...ahhhhhhhhhh," he screamed when she grabbed his crotch and began to squeeze hard.

He raised his hand like he was going to hit her.

"Hit me and I will rip your nuts out and feed them to you." She released him and he staggered away. "I had five older brothers and he thinks a little girl can't take care of herself," she muttered under her breath.

I was laughing so hard my sides hurt. "Okay, let's go out to the beach. I don't want to talk in here."

We went to the shore, and I told her about what I had overheard at the clubhouse and explained I wanted to meet with her, Sherry, Dave, Kenny and Roger.

She looked at me. "That's only six counting you. If you find yourself in trouble that isn't a very large group."

"I'm no great believer in 'the more the merrier' idea and power in numbers just doesn't work all the time. The fewer people involved in this, the less chance there is of someone allowing something to slip. Besides it has to be people I trust," I told her.

She looked me right in the eyes. "So I'm one you trust."

"Yes, I trust you because I know you would not intentionally say or do something that would get me hurt." I smiled at her. "Besides, I think a 'little girl' like you might be handy if the fighting gets in close."

CHAPTER ELEVEN

I left North Beach and decided to make a run by the clubhouse. Instead of going straight out Padre Island Drive, I dropped down from the bridge and headed for the bay. I cruised down Shoreline Blvd past the "T" and "L" heads and worked my way across to Staples cruising toward the drive. I took a few back streets and then pulled in front of the club house. There were a dozen bikes out front, and I could hear the jukebox blasting; Kenny was there but I didn't see Casper's machine. I strolled in to a welcome from all the brothers; some of them I hadn't seen in the months I had been home. In thirty minutes it was like the old days; everyone drinking and enjoying the fellowship that happens here.

I had a pretty good buzz going when Kenny pulled me aside. "This is what you want to ruin, man? You want to see all this go away?"

"Kenny, I want this to continue. I want to see this club thriving because brothers are together, not destroyed by a few assholes selling drugs. Casper has to be stopped, and if Eddie is in on it, like I know he is, he goes down too. Then someone takes the lead who really wants this club to be what it used to be," I told him.

"I suppose that someone is you," he said, his eyes narrowing.

"I'm not the club pres, never wanted to be and still don't. I'm not a leader, but you, or others can be," I responded.

Kenny stood there for a minute. "I have a lot of thinking to do."

"Will you be there tomorrow?" I asked.

"I don't know yet. Don't push me, man. I need to think this through when I have my head straight," he answered as he walked away.

"I won't say anything else about it, but I hope I see you there," I told him.

I stayed a little while longer then headed out; I needed some air. The bike felt good and the night was cool as I cruised through the darkness. I was deep into the ride when I noticed bike lights a long distance behind me. I kept an eye on them, watching them getting larger. I rolled the throttle to put some distance between us and kept it open; the bike was pushing one-fifteen when I went into the curve then I grabbed the brakes hard and almost lost it as I threw the bike into a side street. I ran hard and pulled a right then dumped my lights. I listened as the bikes approached then blew past without seeing me.

Leaving the lights out I went back to the drive and opened the bike up; soon I was blowing by cars scaring the crap out of unsuspecting motorists. I'm certain they weren't used to being passed by motorcycles at over a hundred with no lights. It didn't take long to catch them, and I waited until I was right on top of them before my lights blazed on. Two of the riders I recognized as Casper's friends, the other was a rough looking Latino powerhouse.

I rolled up beside them and pulled the .45 from my belt, aiming it at the lead biker. He slammed on the brakes, causing the second rider to clip the first, and the bikes went out of control. I stuffed the gun back in my belt and twisted the throttle hard.

The first chance I got, I did a one-eighty and cruised back by the bikes. They were on the side of the road but no one appeared to be injured. I certainly wasn't going to hang around for a long discussion, but I did get close enough to get a good look at all three men then shot on down the road.

I turned off Padre Island Drive and headed for the Blue Note, parking around back so as not to advertise my presence. I walked straight back to Sherry's office, knocked and called Sherry by name. She came to the door and hugged me when she saw me then stood back. "You look a hell of a lot better than you did the last time I saw you"

I walked into the office. "Thanks, Sherry, I feel a lot better than I have in a while. Do you have a minute?"

"For you, any time. What's up?" she said as she sat behind her desk.

I pulled a chair around so we could talk without the desk between us. "Sherry, you know a little of what is going on but you don't know it all. Before I tell you about this though you have to know that just by telling you the whole story I am bringing you into a situation that could be dangerous."

She poured us both a cup of coffee. "TJ, Jean Marie called me earlier and said you may be coming by. She also told me pretty much the same thing you just did. My answer to her was that if she needed me, I'm right here. I am telling you the same thing right now. So open up, tell me the whole story. Before we start, have you thought about Roger as well?"

The coffee she handed me resembled tar, both in taste and consistency. "I will talk to him later. I'm pretty sure he'll be in."

"He's in the bar. Do you want me to get him?"

I thought for a minute. "Might as well."

She left the office, and I quickly poured the coffee out and grabbed a Pepsi from her fridge. A few minutes later they both came into the room. I looked up at Roger. "I guess you wonder why I called this meeting."

Roger laughed. "Probably because you haven't been getting enough attention lately," he said as he grasped my hand.

For the next twenty minutes I went through the whole story, explaining every detail I could and every hazard I could think of. It was so quiet in the room that I could hear each of us breathe. It was Roger who broke the silence. "I knew something was up but I never expected anything like this. I can't believe you kept all this to yourself."

I looked down examining the floor. "I couldn't say anything, Roger; I had to keep this as quiet as possible."

"So, what changed?" Sherry asked.

I looked at Roger. "Actually it was you," I said to him. "You were the one who finally convinced me that hanging on this thing alone was a bad idea. Look, if either or both of you are not up for this, I'm cool with it. I'll move out of your place, Roger, and I will walk away from the Blue Note."

He immediately responded. "No, I'm in and the place is yours as long as you want it. What do you want from us, or at least from me?"

Sherry looked at me and just nodded.

"For now I want both of you to think about this. There is a meeting at the apartment tomorrow at five. Right now none of the people I have invited know who the others are. If you are up for it, be there; otherwise just don't show up."

"I'll be there. My mind is already made up," said Sherry.

"You know I'm in," Roger chimed in.

I sat there drinking my Pepsi. "Okay, I need to touch base with one more person then I can call it a night," I said as I headed for the door. "I'll see you guys tomorrow, unless you change your mind."

I figured I better hit the side roads on the way home—if those guys were still able they would be looking for me. I rolled onto the property and into the garage. No one knew where I was staying except the people I had told, so I felt safe enough. I went into the apartment and dialed Dave's number. I briefly explained what was happening and told him about the meeting; he said he would be there.

Finally I could relax and call it a night. My stomach reminded me that food had not been part of my day, and I knew there were a couple of steaks in the freezer. I pulled them out and threw both of them in the oven and allowed them to thaw then spiced them up and put them in the broiler. I poured a healthy drink and realized the pain was rolling through my body. I popped a couple of pain pills and sat back waiting for the steaks to get done. I was fighting sleep from the booze, pills and a tired body; it seemed to take forever for the meat to get done. When they were done just the way I liked them I sat down and devoured them. When I was through I lay on the couch to finish watching a show on television but I was asleep in a matter of minutes. I awoke at two in the morning, went back to the bedroom and fell on the bed.

Ten in the morning I awoke to the smell of coffee brewing and bacon cooking so I stumbled to the kitchen. Roger was just taking bacon from the pan and dropping three eggs in. "Over easy, right, TJ?"

"You got it, bro. What the hell are you doing here?"

"Fixing you breakfast. I know you haven't been eating right, and we need to get you back in shape. After we eat and you have a little time to let it settle, we are going to the gym," he said.

The bacon was crisp, the eggs perfect and the coffee out of this world. After an hour we went to his gym, a room in his house that had everything you could ask for in a gym. For the next two hours he tortured me, taking me through paces I had forgotten existed. When we were through we went into the sauna and sat for twenty minutes talking about nothing special.

He was quiet for a few seconds. "TJ, I'm worried about you."

"Worried about me? What the hell for?" I asked.

He looked down at his hands, sweat pouring from his head. "You've gotten yourself into a pretty tight mess here with some people who aren't going to hesitate to take you out."

"I'm still a member of CC Riders. It isn't easy to take out a brother without some people getting upset and starting to look for blood themselves," I told him with more confidence than I felt. Of course I hadn't told him about the three bikers last night.

"Right! Remember you are talking about busting some of those same brothers and you haven't been around them lately. Who do you think they'll back when it comes down to it?" he asked.

I got up and left the sauna, the heat was starting to get to me, and Roger followed. We sat in the gym cooling off. "You have a point. I know you, Roger, you aren't telling me this without a suggestion."

"Do you have anyone in the club you can trust completely?" he asked.

"I can let you know that this afternoon. If Kenny shows up the answer is yes; if not I'm pretty much on my own. I mean I trust most of these guys with my life, but would they take my word over Eddie's? I'm not that confident. If Kenny comes along we might be able to work the inside but without him I'm pretty much the Lone Ranger in this," I told him.

He sat there looking at me. "You really are in deep, aren't you?"

"I guess I am, and if every single person I asked to come over this afternoon doesn't show, I'm in deep shit with no shovel," I replied.

He clapped me on the back. "Well, no matter what happens I'm here and anything I have is yours, including money, and don't be afraid to ask for it. Let's hit the showers before we start attracting the local water buffalo."

It was after two by the time I got out of the shower and dressed. My body still felt a little shaky but all in all I felt pretty good. I automatically reached for the pain pills then took inventory—I didn't hurt enough for them and I doubted I had for a while. I went into the bathroom and started to dump them down the toilet then changed my mind and put them in the medicine cabinet. I needed my head clear and I was sure those and the booze weren't helping.

I left the bike in the garage and pulled the Pontiac out and headed nowhere in particular. I ended up on Padre Island Drive and was soon passed by one of Casper's buddies. I kicked up the speed a little but stayed back a ways, hoping he wouldn't see me. He turned onto Military Run and passed the old airfield going away from town. The traffic was sparse on the road but I managed to keep a truck between the bike and me until he turned onto an unpaved road. I couldn't follow him without him seeing the dust cloud behind him. I found a place to turn around and looked along the roadside then headed for home.

On the way to the house I stopped at a Shell station and picked up an area map. I hadn't been back in that area since I was in high school and had no clue what was back in that area. I walked into the kitchen, laid out the map on the table, and marked where I had been when he turned off. From what I could tell, that area was either undeveloped property or farm land. Why was he going back in there? It wasn't a scenic ride and the road looked like it was not great for traveling on a street bike. Was it possible they had their meth lab set up back there away from everything? It made sense but how was anyone going to be able to get near it—the dust would be a giveaway if anyone went down that road. I wrote down the information so I wouldn't lose it and marked the time.

Roger showed up at four-thirty with a load of barbecue with all the fixings. "What the hell is this?" I asked.

"Look, just because we are meeting for business doesn't mean we can't eat while we talk," he responded.

I couldn't argue with that logic. We sat there for a few minutes then I looked at him. "Roger, you don't have to get into this mess. For that matter I probably shouldn't be including you or Sherry in this thing. It would destroy me if either of you got hurt."

He laughed. "And what about your other friends? Are you telling me they don't mean anything to you?"

"You know better than that," I told him. "I am

very concerned for Dave—if anything happened Maria would be left alone. As for Kenny, it's his club too, and no matter how much he protests he wants the club back the way it used to be. I'm not sure how far he's willing to go to make that happen. Jean Marie has a job to do and I know she'll do pretty much whatever it takes. The thing is I haven't known you and Sherry very long; we aren't long lost friends with a deep past together. To a very great degree you don't have a dog in this hunt."

"So let me get this straight," he said. "We haven't known you for long so we should just bail out and let you just swing in the wind? That makes as much sense as the rest of this conversation."

"You have a great way of turning everything I say into something I don't intend it to mean. I don't want anyone to get hurt; that is why I have been going this alone."

He looked at me thoughtfully. "If this thing goes sour your friends will probably get hurt anyway. By including us it at least gives some options and a few more heads to help prevent any mistakes. Let us worry about our end of this. Just keep us in the loop so we know what's going on so we know when to duck."

About that time Sherry pulled up with Jean Marie right behind her. Well, that was two anyway. A few minutes later Dave came rolling up in his old truck. Everyone came in and we sat around devouring the food and downing cold ones while just bullshitting.

"Okay," I finally said, "it's almost twenty after. I was hoping Kenny would show up but I guess he made his decision. All of you know a pretty good part of what is happening but if we get to point and you want to pull out, just say so, no hard feelings."

Nobody moved. Just then I heard a motorcycle pulling up the drive, and I recognized the sound of Kenny's ride.

I went to the door and opened it to find Kenny walking up the sidewalk. "I'm here, bro, but no promises except that no one will know about this."

I took a few minutes to introduce everyone and give a brief rundown on each. "I tried not to involve anyone in this; it's my problem and my intent was to handle it but someone here called me an idiot. At this point, the people in this room are the only ones I know I can trust, and I can assure each of you can do the same. From now on there are no secrets in this group when it comes to this mess because anything can be important to someone else in the group."

I laid out the whole thing, went as deeply as I could and made sure everyone understood why I was doing this. It was Dave who had the first question. "So, what do you want me to do?"

I looked at my old friend. "Just what you have been doing, plus a little more. Your place will be a drop if anyone needs to touch base with someone else in the group. We will all have everyone else's contact numbers but memorize them and don't carry them on you. Dave, you need to keep an eye on the traffic to and from the island, plus the clubhouse is close by and I need you to keep an eye out for activity there. We don't know where they are making the stuff or who they are delivering it to—maybe we can get some idea."

"You got it, man, whatever you need, but can't we just call one another on the phone?" he asked.

I looked at the entire group. "The less direct contact we have about this the better off we are. Sooner or later we could be seen together in a situation that may seem suspicious so drops at Dave's will keep things out of sight.

"TJ, I still have a problem with busting brothers," Kenny said. "It just doesn't seem right."

It was Jean Marie who responded. "Kenny, I don't want to see anyone go down for this who isn't directly involved. I understand how you feel about your brothers. Cops feel the same way about one another, but I would burn a bad one in a heartbeat. Further, anyone who helps us will be protected as best we can."

Kenny shook his head. "TJ, you've always been stand-up, and nothing against you, Jean Marie, but I have had a belly full of cops and I have never met a straight one, never met one I could trust."

Sherry walked over to Kenny. "You have now. I've known Jean Marie for more years than either one of us care to admit. The only illegal thing I have ever seen her do is smoke a joint and even that was kind of my fault—I talked her into it."

Jean Marie spoke up next. "Kenny, I want to get something off the street that is killing people. Look at your girlfriend—if you can't get her help soon, you will be paying for her funeral. If we shut these guys down, we will make a deep cut in the product on the streets here in Corpus Christi. I promise you this, too—any time you can get Shauna to commit, I'll personally make sure she gets the best care possible."

Kenny looked at her. "I'm gonna hold you to that. So TJ, what's my part in this?"

I sat there for a minute. "Casper is avoiding you like the plague. He knows you want a piece of him for what happened to Shauna so I don't expect Eddie to just open up and tell you where he is but you might catch a clue. Also, talk down Casper for what he did.

Get a line on anyone who may be working with him."

Kenny had a thoughtful look on his face. "There are a few of the guys who are truly pissed about Casper selling drugs, charged up about him shooting Shauna, and they think Eddie should put a stop to it. Maybe I can work some of them."

Roger chimed in. "Be careful, Kenny; these guys probably play for keeps."

"He's right, Kenny," I told him. "Be careful and no matter how much you trust them, keep them in the dark about this group and keep me in the loop about what is going on."

Sherry spoke up next. "Where am I in this?"

"I just need you to keep covering my back. If I am supposed to be at work and someone is looking for me, you have to keep me aware of who is looking for me. I don't want you deep in this thing but you deserved to know the whole story," I explained.

Roger looked at me. "That just leaves me."

I turned to him. "I need something big from you bro. I need a place close to the clubhouse but far enough away that they wouldn't see me come and go. Can you find us a place there somewhere and cover the cost?"

"Give me the address of the clubhouse; if there is anything there I'll find it," he said. I wrote down the address and gave it to him.

We went to the map and I explained what had happened earlier, and I told them I needed to know what was there. Roger was the one who explained. "That is nothing land, most of the area is sand and sea grass. Nothing else grows there except jack rabbits and rattlesnakes."

Jean Marie came over. "I'll get the day shift supervisor to send a car out there to take a look."

Roger shook his head. "Oh yeah, that would really work."

"Then what?" she asked.

"Look," Roger continued. "I have a friend who has a small plane. I'm sure I can get him to take me up and we can fly around the area."

I thought about it. "If you're sure you can trust him. That sounds like the best idea yet. When you make the run let me know what you find."

We all talked about various ideas and then called it a day. I felt a lot better when we were through. I felt like we were making headway, and I didn't feel alone.

CHAPTER TWELVE

I needed some time to just get away and breathe so I hit the road up over the high rise and down into North Beach. I cruised on down to Blasters. Carl was at his usual place; he poured me a drink as I slid up to the bar.

"Man, you got some balls coming in here. There is a certain fellow who would like a piece of your girlfriend," he said.

I looked around the bar. "Well, I don't see her here so I guess he's safe enough."

Carl laughed the looked at me quizzically. "So, what's up with you and the cop anyway?"

I looked shocked. "Cop? What are you talking about?"

"Come on, man, don't bullshit me. I been in this town since I was born. There ain't a cop on the street I don't know," he said confidently.

"Who else knows?" I asked.

He chuckled. "I doubt anyone does. I happened to see her about a year ago. She's a pretty easy face to remember."

Just then the door opened and the smile was gone from his face.

"Well, is this our little cracker? Where is that little bitch at? I got somethin' for her," he said as he grabbed his crotch.

"Really? I would think you would be hiding that thing just in case she comes out of the bathroom."

His gaze shot at the door marked Ladies. "Well, it seems your little girlfriend isn't here to protect your ass right now," he said as he walked closer.

"I don't need her protection any more than she needed mine when she put you on your knees begging her to let go," I chided as I slipped from the barstool.

Carl moved from behind the bar, his baseball bat at the ready. "You two better just cool down or I will take you both out." He looked at the other man. "Are you here to drink or fight?"

The black guy started to push his finger into my chest but before it got that far I grabbed it and twisted hard, driving him right to his knees. I looked down at him. "You need to stay away from me and my friends, you're gonna wear holes in the knees of your pants," then let him go.

He got up, walked to the old pool table and threw down a quarter. "Are you as good at shootin' pool as you are at shootin' off your mouth?"

Carl looked at me and shook his head, but I took my drink and headed for the table. "I'm not good but I like a little fun now and again. Are we just playing for freebies or would you like to spend your money on my drinks?"

He threw the rack toward my end of the table. "Rack 'em and break out your wallet."

For the next few minutes we shot pool then at one point he was standing next to me. "You're TJ, right?" he asked.

"If that's any of your business I would like to know why," I responded.

"Look man, I work with some of the same people you work with. My name is Lawrence but all my friends call me Hack," he told me.

I leaned over and dropped the five ball in the side

pocket setting up the eight. "Well, Lawrence, I have no clue who you could be talking about. I'm a bouncer—"

"At the Blue Note, I know that, but I mean the other people you work for," he said as I banked the eight off the side rail straight into the corner pocket.

"Don't know what you're talking about," I said as I tossed the cue on the table then turned to Carl. "Adios," and headed for the door. I made a mental note to have this turkey checked out and if he was working for those "other people" I would see if I could have him shot.

I rolled out of the lot and headed north, once again toward Port Aransas. I hadn't been back since the night…well, in a while. I was kicked back, feeling good, when the motorcycle cop pulled up and hit his reds and siren; I immediately looked at my speedometer, for once I was cruising at the speed limit, well, close to it anyway. I pulled over and pulled my wallet out.

"Driver's license and registration please," said the cop with a not too convincing note of authority in his voice.

The stupid ass couldn't see them held out toward him in my left hand. "You mean these, officer?" I said in a sarcastic tone.

He took them from my hand. "Don't be such a smartass, son; it will get you nowhere but free room and board as a guest of the state."

"Sorry, sir." I get a little testy with these harassment stops. "Now will you just tell me what I was doing that took you away from your donuts?" I really was feeling testy, although I was not being very smart.

"I stopped you for ignoring a brother," he said as he removed his helmet. It was Jimmy Talbot. Jimmy joined the club right after it was formed; we called him Thirteen because he was the thirteenth member of CC Riders. He was older than most of the members and was going to college at Del Mar at the time. He left the club a year after I joined the Navy; I never really knew why.

"When did you start working for The Man?" I asked.

He laughed a little. "That's why I had to leave the club. It wouldn't exactly look good on my resume."

"I guess not. So how did you know it was me?" I asked, truly puzzled.

"My sister-in-law told me about you. Seems she spent the night with you out on Mustang Island," he said. "I was surprised to hear you were back in town."

"Sandy is your sister-in-law? Wait, in order to have a sister-in-law you would have to find someone hard up enough to marry you," I responded completely amazed.

"Yeah, on both counts. Sandy told me all about her night with you, well not everything, but enough I could guess the rest. When she started describing the man she had met, I knew it was you before she finished and she described your bike to a T," he said.

"I'm surprised she even remembered me; we didn't exactly part ways with a smile," I told him.

"Yeah, well, she thinks she may have made a mistake there. She would like to find you; she's driven all over Corpus looking for you."

"I'm not so sure it was a mistake, Jimmy."

"Why, you in some kind of trouble?" he asked.

I looked at him thoughtfully. "Not like you might

be thinking, but yeah I am and she doesn't need to be a part of it."

"Tell me about it. What is it? We're still brothers after all," he prodded.

"Well, you might still be riding but you're getting paid for it, and that isn't exactly a bike we want to be seen around. Honestly, I might like to tell you about it but this isn't the place or the time," I explained.

"I get off a little after midnight; could we talk then?"

I thought about it. "I'll be down the Island a few miles. Ice down a six and meet me out there if you are serious."

He responded immediately. "I'm serious, I'll be there. You were one of the good guys, TJ. You played tough but you played fair."

"Okay, bro, see ya in a bit. Get back to work before all your donuts spoil," I told him as I stepped across the saddle. Just for grins I dumped the clutch, throwing dust and rocks at him as I screamed down the road.

It was still early so when I saw a bar with a couple of bikes out front I pulled into the parking lot. As I walked in I noticed the bar was about half white and half Latino. I went up to the bar and ordered a beer then turned with my back to the bar and leaned there looking over the crowd. A big darker skinned Latino walked over to me. "Dude, you're TJ, aren't you?"

I looked at him closely—he was tall, probably thirty and looked like his muscles were about to rip his shirt apart; he was certainly someone I think I would remember but I didn't recognize him at all. "Yeah, and who are you?"

"My name is Rudy Espinosa," he said as he offered his hand. "Maria is my younger sister, you know, the one who married Dave. I remember you from when you jumped in and saved his ass."

I wasn't real comfortable here; first I was pretty much outnumbered, second this guy didn't look like he was about to offer me a beer, and third the only weapons I had with me were not easy to get to without being obvious. "Look, Dave and Maria are doing pretty well from what I've seen, and unless there's something I don't know about, I think Dave has done pretty well by her."

He was standing so close I could almost tell what he had for lunch. "I don't have a problem with Dave, and I don't have a problem with you jumpin' into that stuff. As a matter of fact that is the reason I haven't started kicking your ass."

I was getting a little more than concerned, but I tried to be as casual as possible as I took a drink from my beer then hooked the thumb of my right hand into my right hip pocket where I kept the little 380. I turned back to him. "I don't understand what your beef with me is then. I haven't done anything to you, Dave or Maria."

"No, you haven't done anything to them, or even me. It's my brother Jesse you are messing with," he said, his voice getting louder and his energy level rising.

"Hold it, man. Back off and let me breathe and tell me what the hell I have done to Jesse. To be honest with you I don't even know him!" I said, defending myself.

"Your club, man! Your club is forcing him to buy their meth and sell it," he said getting angrier.

I was none too happy either and, for a moment,

forgot about the fact that this guy could probably take me apart. "Look, your brother deals drugs. No one makes him do a damned thing in the first place and in the second place I have nothing to do with drugs and I don't know anything about the club selling to anyone else," I said not being completely truthful.

He looked at me like he wasn't buying a bit of it. "That's bullshit. You tryin' to tell me the Riders are dealing and you ain't part of it? You know nothin' about what they're doin'. Sell that to someone who might buy it. Jesse was threatened—they said they would cut our mother's throat after they raped her if he didn't deal their shit."

I slowly moved my hand away from my pocket and stood there for a minute. "Rudy, I need to ask you a favor, but first I am going to tell you something but I can't talk with so many people standing around."

He stared straight into my eyes, never blinking. "I may not be the smartest person in the world, but I'm not stupid enough to let you trick me into getting me alone so you can try to kick my ass."

"Rudy, I have no intention of getting into a scrap with you. I know you could take me and even if you didn't I would have to face your family and I certainly don't want that. I want no problems with Dave's family."

It seemed he stood there thinking for a long time then turned and said something in Spanish to the bartender who answered and pointed toward the back. "Come on, but I mean it—you screw with me and if I don't take you apart someone else will." We walked back into the storage room behind the bar. "Okay, what is it that is so secret?"

"I can't tell you everything, Rudy, but I do know the club is involved with meth. I'm trying to find out what is going on and who is involved," I explained.

"You're telling me that you, a member of the club, expect me to believe that you don't know what's going on and you're tryin' to do something about it?" he asked.

"I guess if I were on the other side of this thing I would have my doubts too," I said, thinking. "Look, Rudy, you don't really know me but I have always been stand-up. I stepped into the middle of the mess with Dave even knowing I was greatly outnumbered. I love Maria like a sister; I have no desire to hurt her or anyone in her family."

He considered this a moment. "So, what is Jesse supposed to do? He can't just stop or they will hurt our family."

I thought for a minute, "I need to talk to Jesse. I'll be back in Corpus tomorrow. Can you set up a meeting?"

He leaned back. "Okay, TJ, I'm going to trust you, but I swear on my father's grave that if you hurt my family I'll find you and you will never get the chance to do that again. I can get Jesse to meet you at Dave's tomorrow, say one in the afternoon."

"Good. I'll be there. If I'm not there right at one tell him to hang out there. I promise Rudy, I am on the level and I'll do my damndest to get Jesse out of this," I said.

"Okay, man, you got one shot," he replied as he walked toward the door.

I walked out behind him, went to the bar and finished my beer then headed for the exit. I could feel eyes on my back and knew that if Rudy had said the word I would be found in the parking lot looking like I had been mauled by wolves.

I got on the bike and pointed it toward Mustang

Island. As soon as I hit the sand I began thinking about Sandy; confusing thoughts were screaming through my head. I wanted her but I feared for her at the same time. So far no one had been hurt but I knew it was just a matter of time.

I stopped at the small grocery and got a cold one to hold me over until Jimmy got there then headed down the beach. It was close to an hour before I saw a single headlight coming my way. Jimmy looked more like himself in street clothes and riding the same old knuckle head I remembered from years ago. Jimmy was about six foot six and not a small man at all, though I doubt you could find much fat on his two hundred plus frame. Seeing him step off the bike brought memories back of the way his large frame dwarfed the bike.

Jimmy walked over, dropped onto the sand beside me and handed me a beer. We sat in silence for a minute then Jimmy broke the silence. "Okay, bro, so tell me about it."

I told him pretty much the whole story as we sat there enjoying the beer. When I was through with the story he opened another beer. "You really do have a problem, don't you?"

"You know, you grasp the obvious pretty well for a cop," I responded.

"So, it's true that the Riders are cooking and selling meth. I had heard that but I just figured it was all talk," he said, "I never figured Eddie for the type who would allow that in the club."

"Allow it? He is the one behind it all. He is the one who has pulled it all together from what I can find out. Between him and Casper, they're running the whole show."

"So, what can I do, bro?" he asked.

"I don't know Jimmy. If you got involved with this thing you could be risking your job. Plus I have enough people putting their asses on the line—I don't want anyone to get hurt, but the more people involved the greater the risk," I told him.

"Look, TJ, you've put your ass on the line for a lot of people and serving in Viet Nam you have put it on the line more than a few times. As for Sandy, she is a big girl—be straight with her and let her make her own decisions."

I smiled. "It isn't just that. She is a reporter. I can't allow her to know too much and let anything slip."

He was smiling now. "Sandy is pretty ambitious but she is no dummy. I can't speak for her but I can't imagine she would release anything and get people hurt."

"But just being around this mess could get her hurt and I couldn't allow that," I told him.

"I know what you mean, and if it was anyone else I would be concerned, but I know you, TJ, and I know she would be as safe with you as anywhere. Again, she's a big girl, let her make her own decisions."

We sat there in silence for a few more minutes just drinking our beer. "Well, if I run across her again I'll think about it. For now, though, I need to head back and see if anything has come up."

"TJ, if you need anything," he began writing on a card, "you have my home phone and the number for the unit I work out of. Just tell them who you are. I'll leave word for them to put you through."

I took the card and looked at it in the bright moonlight. "What is the third number?" I asked.

He smiled. "That's Sandy's number, just in case you decide you would like to touch base with her."

I put the card in my pocket. "I don't think it would be wise to call her, but I'll keep that in mind." We shook hands and headed for the bikes. We rode together until we reached Ingleside where he turned off.

The rest of the ride home I couldn't kick the feeling that something was wrong, and I rolled the throttle hard as I pointed the bike toward Corpus. I decided to head for Dave's so I swung around toward Padre Island Drive and opened the bike up again.

When I pulled behind the building I was surprised to see Dave at the door coming toward me yelling something that was drowned out by the big bike's engine. I shut down the bike and stepped off. "TJ, that lady cop, Jean Marie, has been trying to get ahold of you. Something has happened but she wouldn't tell me what."

I ran into the bait shop and grabbed the phone, trying every number I could—no answers anywhere so I called Roger but got the same thing. Finally I called Sherry. When she came to the phone I almost yelled into the phone. "Sherry, have you seen Jean Marie?"

She was slow to answer. "She was here earlier but she said she was looking for you. Where are you?"

"At Dave's."

"Okay, stay there and I will find her."

"Alright, I'll be here. Do you have any idea what is going on?" I asked.

"Just stay there, Jean Marie will find you," she responded then hung up the phone.

It was a half hour before Jean Marie got there. I ran out the door. "What the hell is going on?" I screamed.

She looked at me, tears starting to fill her eyes. "It's Roger."

CHAPTER THIRTEEN

I stood there stunned. "What happened? What's wrong?"

"His truck was found on a side road off Military Highway. We have torn that area apart but we haven't found him," she said.

"Where on Military?"

"At the far end, well past the airfield. It isn't anywhere near the road you told us about, that was the first thing we thought about," she said. "You look like you need some sleep. Go on home and I'll call you there if we find anything."

After she left I sat there with Dave. "Look, I won't be coming around again for a while. It looks like Roger may be in trouble and I don't want you involved."

"Look, man, everyone already knows we're friends, so not coming around isn't going to change a thing. I'm going to be right here so you come by any time; don't stay away. I need to know you're okay, TJ," he said.

I told him about my run in with Rudy. "I am already causing problems."

"Don't sweat Rudy. I'll clear the air with him and before you even say it, I won't tell him anything."

"Dave, I didn't know anything about the club pressing Jesse to sell drugs. When this is over, I'll make sure Jesse is taken care of. We'll get him into a real job and he can stop selling that crap."

I got to the bike and fired it up, just about to head for the house then decided to run by the clubhouse. Eddie's bike was sitting right up front along with a few others, including Kenny's. I parked the bike, went into the clubhouse and grabbed a beer. I saw Kenny across the room and was about to go over to him when he gave a slight shake of his head before turning back to the biker he was talking to.

Eddie came over and slapped me on the back. "Haven't seen you around for a couple of days."

It took everything I had to stop myself from grabbing him and choking him until he told me where Roger was. "Just been cruising around trying to decide what I want to do. The job at the Blue Note really isn't covering the bills," I told him.

"I told you, come on by the shop. I have plenty of work and a serious lack of good mechanics I can trust. I know damned good and well some of these guys are rippin' me off," he said.

I thought for a minute. "I would love to, man, but Sherry needs me out at the bar."

"That's cool. The shop closes by five most days and you can still get out there whenever you need to. I mean it, I can pay you good and you won't be killing yourself, plus I can get away from the shop if I have someone there I can trust," he was almost pleading.

"I'll stop by tomorrow and talk some more. Maybe I can work there two or three days a week." This would give me a chance to get closer to Eddie, and this was perfect because he was the one asking me—I wasn't doing something to try to work my way inside. I walked over to the pool table and began racking up the balls and saw Kenny coming my way.

"Up for a game?" I asked.

"Sure, I always like winning," he said with a smile. We played for a while then Kenny came over next to me. "What's up, man? You look bummed about something?"

"Roger has disappeared. They found his truck but couldn't find him. Look, you better stay away from me. They are sure to tie me to Roger; then it's just a quick jump to tie you in," I told him as I racked the balls again.

Later he came over next to me again. "No way, man, we are in this together, all the way," he said as he dropped the eight ball by mistake and began racking the balls again.

I stood next to him. "Okay, but we need to get Shauna away from here. Is there somewhere you can send or take her?"

He thought for a minute. "My sister lives in San Antonio. She likes Shauna and would take her in a heartbeat."

"Good, do it tonight. I need to get some sleep and do some thinking. I have to find Roger," I told him.

We played a while longer then Kenny grabbed his jacket. "Okay, I'm outta here. I'm gonna get Shauna and get out of Corpus. I'll see you when I get back," and he blew out the door.

A few minutes later I left and headed for the apartment, the whole time watching the road behind me. I went into the apartment, and when I went to the fridge to get a beer I found a note and some keys next to the beer. There were two sets of house keys and some car keys. I opened the note:

"TJ, I found a house for you. The address is on the tag attached to the keys. It's an old two story and from the upstairs you can see the front of the clubhouse clearly. There is also a set of house keys to my place. I meant to give them to you a while back but kept forgetting. The other keys are to a couple of cars in the garage and there is a set for an old truck that is parked in the garage at the other house. You should be able to come and go in that truck pretty easily. Okay, now that takes care of what you asked me to do. Now I need to tell you something else.

"Until I met you, I was just chugging along headed for my grave. I have cancer and I really shouldn't be alive right now, but because of you I do feel alive again. Sherry knows about it, that's part of why we became such good friends. I don't have any family to speak of and I want someone to enjoy what I have spent my life building up; here is where you come in. Sherry won't take anything from me, so I've made arrangements with my lawyer so that when it is my time you'll have everything I own including life insurance, investments, property and cash but my demand on you is to take care of Sherry. Make sure she and Andria never need for anything.

"Now, a friend and I are going to see what we can find at the trailer so if you don't see me by morning, it means we are unable to return. TJ, don't look for retribution for anything, just take care of the business you started. Okay, I'm out of here, you take care and hopefully I will see you in the morning."

Now I was scared. Surely they hadn't parked that far from the trailer and walked—that had to be six or eight miles from the truck to where the road to the trailer was. I thought for a minute and looked at my watch; it was after two in the morning. I decided to see if Sherry was still at the Blue Note; she answered the phone right away. "Sherry, this is TJ."

"Have you heard anything from Roger?" she asked immediately.

I tried to respond calmly. "No, I haven't seen him."

"He said he would call tonight after…" her voice trailed off.

"Sherry, after what? You knew he was going somewhere tonight? Why the hell didn't you tell me!" I screamed into the phone.

"He made me promise not to say anything. I know it was wrong but he made me promise and now I'm afraid for him." She began crying.

"I am going to find him, Sherry. Wherever he is I'm going to find him, but I need a favor right now."

"Anything, TJ, what do you need?" she asked.

"I need you to come get me. I'm at the apartment and I need to go somewhere, but I don't want to leave my bike there. Just come by and get me."

"But what about Roger?"

"One thing at a time. This is part of what I need to do to look for him," I explained.

"Okay, I'll be right over. Everything is done here," she said then hung up the phone.

It seemed like only a couple of minutes before she rolled up to the front door. I ran out and jumped in her car and told her where to go.

The house was not new, but it looked to be in pretty good shape. It had a two-car garage so I opened one of the doors to discover an old '55 Chevy pickup. I opened the other door and told her to pull her truck inside. She got out of her truck and we went into the house and up the stairs.

"Who's truck is that?" she asked.

"Roger bought it and left it here for me," I said as we got upstairs and went to the back of the house. We could see clearly to the clubhouse and right now the only bike there was Eddie's. I wished I had a pair of binoculars, but I could see pretty clearly.

She came up next to me. "Okay, I got you here. Now what about Roger?"

"Sherry, right now we don't know anything except his truck was found out on Military," I told her.

"What the hell was he doing out there? Come on, TJ, you said we are in this thing together. Now be straight with me," she demanded.

"I want you out of it, Sherry. This is getting a little too rough, and I don't want to see anyone else getting hurt." I cussed myself knowing I had just screwed up.

"Anyone else? That's what you said, 'anyone else.' What are you talking about? You aren't telling me everything and I want to know right now! Quit screwing around," she said, her voice getting louder.

I sat on the floor, my head hanging. "I honestly don't know anything except that he and a friend went to see about that old trailer. I didn't know anything about it until I got back to the apartment tonight. Don't be yelling at me about not telling everything— how long have you known that Roger is sick?"

Now it was her head that dropped. "Almost as long as I've known him. He was diagnosed over a year ago, but it is aggressive and they didn't even give him a year. TJ, he made me promise; he said he didn't want to be left out of this. He wanted to do what he could."

I heard the rumble of a motorcycle and looked up to see Casper pulling into the clubhouse lot. Before he could get off the bike Eddie came out and was very animated, seemed angry about something. As Casper stepped from the bike Eddie threw a roundhouse that connected on the side of Casper's face hard enough to drop him to the ground. Three other bikes rolled into the lot and the riders jumped off to separate the two men who were rolling around on the ground. At one point two of the men were holding Eddie when Casper broke away and hit the big man twice before the others intervened.

I looked at Sherry. "You need to get out of here."

"I'm not going anywhere until you tell me what you think you are going to do," she said.

I thought for a moment. "I'm going to crash here for the night then tomorrow I'm going to touch base with an old friend and see if I can find Roger. I am so tired I can't see straight or I would be doing it now. What I want you to do is get a in touch with Jean Marie and tell her that Roger and another man went to the trailer."

"Nothing stupid, TJ, don't do anything stupid. If you go Lone Ranger on this, I'm gonna go Tonto on your ass," she said without a smile.

"In the first place," I told her, "Tonto was always the one who went into town and got his butt kicked. In the second place Tonto was his trusted companion and in the third place, this is my fight now and I'm about to get about knee deep in it. Now get the hell out of here so I can get some sleep."

She got up, looked at me. "I'll call Jean Marie as soon as I get home, but don't do anything without letting someone know, TJ. I don't want another friend disappearing," then she walked out the door.

The bikers had gone inside the clubhouse, so I lay there on the hardwood floor and closed my eyes; within minutes I was asleep.

The sun was just starting to cast a reddish glow in the sky when I awoke to the sound of the bikes pulling out of the parking lot, all but Eddie's. I got up groggily and staggered down the stairs to the old truck. I got in not knowing what to expect but when I turned the key the sound of a powerful V8 came to life, purring like a kitten. I opened the garage door and backed the truck out, closed the door and drove the short distance to the clubhouse.

As soon as I stepped into the club I knew something was wrong. I looked around the room but couldn't find Eddie. Then I noticed his office door was shut. I tried the knob but it was locked. I yelled for Eddie but didn't hear anything so I kicked the door. It took three hard kicks for it to give. Eddie was on the floor lying in a pool of blood. I went to him and checked for a pulse. It was very weak. I immediately went to the phone and called the local precinct then called Jean Marie's office. No answer.

I went back to Eddie and saw that most of the blood seemed to be coming from a knife wound to his stomach; I applied pressure and waited. A few minutes later the police and an ambulance showed up; the medics worked quickly and got him into the wagon and took off. Before the police could start questioning me, I tried Jean Marie again; this time she answered.

I told her what I had found and where I was. She asked to speak to the sergeant there so I passed him the phone. They spoke a few minutes then he handed the phone back to me. "Go with the sergeant and let him take your statement," she said. "Then get a hold of me and we'll talk."

"Nothin' to talk about. It's time to do some moving. Talking hasn't done a damned thing. I'm going to find Roger," I told her then hung up the phone before she could respond. I didn't have much choice but to go with the cops but at least they allowed me to take the truck and follow them. At one point I thought about splitting but I figured in the long run it would end up slowing me down.

When we got to the cop shop the cops surprised me; they were actually pretty decent. I had expected them to treat me like something they scraped off their shoes. I asked them about Eddie, and they told me he didn't make it to the hospital. I told them about finding Eddie but I didn't tell them about Casper and his friends. I didn't want them to get their hands on him before I did. I needed to take a closer look around the clubhouse, Eddie's house and his shop—there had to be something to tell me more. One of the cops told me I had a phone call and allowed me to take it in one of the offices.

It was Jean Marie. "TJ, what happened?" she asked.

"I don't know. Someone knifed Eddie. He was already on the floor of his office when I got there and no one else was around."

"That's all you know?" she pressed. "You didn't see anything else?"

"Look, I didn't see what happened but I will say this—if I find out before you do I'll be taking care of business."

"TJ, leave this alone. We will find out what happened and take care of it right. Let the proper people handle this the right way," she said somewhat angrily.

"Jean Marie, I have been trying to do it the right way, to allow things to be taken care of properly and now a friend is missing and another dead. Your way is done, now my way starts," I said and started to hang up the phone.

"I know what you're thinking, and looking for revenge will just get you in trouble with the very people you are supposed to be helping. In the end, your ass will end up in jail," she said loudly.

"Look, you do things your way, I'll do them mine and in the end I will take my chances, but I'll have the people who are doing this," I hung up the phone, walked out, got in the truck and left, heading back to the clubhouse.

Inside, I went straight to the office and began going through the desk, pulling every piece out looking for anything that might help. I noticed his club vest hanging on his chair and started looking through it. I found his bike key and two other sets; I put them all in my pocket and headed for the door, jumped in the truck and was just out of the lot when an unmarked car turned the corner and pulled into the lot.

I went back to the apartment, parked the truck in the garage and got on the bike. I sat there for a few minutes and thought about the next step and decided to go to his shop first. The bike felt good and it seemed the fog was lifting a bit. I decided I needed to call Jimmy after I got to the shop.

When I arrived at the shop everything was dark inside. I guessed Eddie hadn't trusted anyone enough to allow them access unless he was around. I quickly found the key, unlocked the door and slipped inside, locking the door behind me. Leaving the lights off I went to the office and found the phone.

I started by calling Jimmy at home and was rewarded first by a very sexy voice. "Talbot residence."

"Hi Mrs. Talbot, this is TJ Hamlin. Is Jimmy home?" I asked.

"The name is Stephanie. I know you TJ. We met a few years ago. Jimmy is out in the garage. I'll get him," she said as she set down the phone.

I heard Jimmy pick up the phone. "What's up, little brother?"

"I'm in trouble, Jimmy, and I need your help," I told him.

"I don't know what I can do, but tell me about it."

I told him everything except what I knew about Casper and his friends. "Jimmy, the main thing I need right now is to find Roger. I'm going to call some of the club together and we will start looking."

"TJ, as your friend and as a member of the Texas Department of Public Safety you know what I have to say. You are going to get yourself in trouble, then it's you standing in front of the judge explaining yourself, so don't go out there ready to burn someone," he warned.

"Jimmy, if you can help, then help. If you can't or won't help then be a friend before being a cop and just stay away," I said then hung up the phone.

I called Kenny and told him to get a hold of all the brothers he trusted and meet me at the clubhouse in an hour. I told him about Eddie, but I would save the rest of the story for the meeting. I then went through all the drawers and cabinets but couldn't find anything. I headed for the bike and took off for Eddie's place. He lived in the same house his father left him when he died, an old run down looking place not far from the shop.

The outside was in serious need of repair, but on the inside there was nothing but the latest and greatest in stereo, television and comfortable furnishings. The bed looked like it hadn't been made in years but I saw nothing special. I went through drawers, closets, the bathroom—any place that might hide a clue to where Roger was. When I ripped off the mattress, I found his stash of drugs, two .45 caliber Colts that I stuffed in my belt, and three thousand in cash. I took it all, not really knowing why. I went through the whole house but didn't find anything else.

The garage told a little story of its own; there were three custom Harleys sitting next to a brand new 'Vette. Two of the bikes were new with almost no mileage; the third was a low rider that was chopped and tricked out to the limit but nothing that helped me.

Back on the bike I headed for the apartment. I only had about twenty minutes before I was to meet Kenny. Once in the apartment I grabbed the little 380s and dropped one in my boot, the other in my vest pocket. I found my seven-inch boot knife and stuffed it in my boot then went to the safe where my guns and ammo were. I pulled the two .45s from my belt and checked them out, both new and looked like they hadn't even been fired. I loaded clips in the two guns then dropped three more loaded clips in my pocket and headed for the door. I looked around the apartment then grabbed a bottle of scotch and stuffed it in my jacket.

I was late so I rolled the bike hard, screaming through the neighborhoods then out on Padre Island Drive. I had just hit ninety when I saw an unmarked car flip around and turn on the lights. I rolled the throttle hard and soon outdistanced the cage far enough to duck into the neighborhood and slipped into the clubhouse parking lot where twenty-five or more bikes stood waiting. I got off the bike and strolled in the door to the clubhouse.

Everyone was talking and milling around until they saw me. I called Kenny up. I took out the bottle and took a big hit from it then handed it to Kenny.

"Okay," I hollered. "Quiet down so I can tell you what's happened and what we are going to do."

"Who put you in charge?" someone yelled.

"Who put me in charge? Look around this room. Do you see anyone who has more time flying these colors than I do? This is not a democracy, leadership isn't elected; with Eddie's death I'm the tallest member left who is still an active member. So for the time being I'm taking over. We'll discuss this other crap later. Anybody else want to challenge me or do we get on with this?" I asked. I looked around the room; it was so quiet you could've heard the proverbial pin drop.

"Okay, for those of you who don't know it, Eddie was murdered sometime before morning today and we are going to get some answers. There are three people we need to find before the cops figure out what is going on. You guys ride in threes, fours or fives and hit any place where Casper and his two buddies might be. When you find them get them back here and keep them here until the whole group is together," I explained.

"Did they do Eddie?" someone screamed.

"Until we have a chance to talk to them they didn't do anything," I told them. "If they put up too much of a fight put them down hard enough so you can get them here. Don't hurt them if you don't have to. There is also a friend of mine missing; he is a large man with dark hair. If you find him, make sure he is okay. His name is Roger."

"What are you going to do?" asked Red.

I looked at the big Irishman. "You, Kenny and I

are going someplace special to look. You carrying?" I asked.

He reached behind him and pulled out a six-inch 357. I asked Kenny and he shook his head. I took one of the .45s from my belt and gave it to him. "Okay, let's go."

CHAPTER FOURTEEN

The roar of bikes filled the air as the parking lot emptied. Red looked at me. "Okay, where are we going?"

"Just follow me and don't get in a big hurry," I said as we rolled toward Padre Island Drive.

I kept us at the legal speed limit until that unmarked car pulled in behind us and hit the lights. This time I didn't think running was a wise move, so I pulled to the shoulder and put the kickstand down. When the guy started getting out of the car I didn't think he was going to ever finish unfolding himself. When he finally did, I realized he was a Texas Ranger by the western cut pants, waist length jacket and the bulge under his jacket where he tried unsuccessfully to hide his canon. He stepped over to me and I looked up at his nearly seven foot height. "That bike is pretty fast—why didn't you run this time?" he asked.

"Sorry, sir, I don't have a clue what you're talking about," I said in my most respectful voice.

He grabbed my vest. "Get in the car."

"Look, I—" I started to say when he pulled me from the bike.

"Get in the car while I'm still feeling friendly," he said pushing me toward the car.

He opened the back door and pushed me in then got into the front. He turned toward me. "Your name is TJ Hamlin, right?" When I didn't answer, he said, "Show me your driver's license."

"Okay, you got me," I said reaching for my wallet and showing him my identification. "So what is it you want?" I asked.

"Look, you must have noticed I didn't frisk you even though I could see the bulge in your jacket so just calm down. Jean Marie wants to talk to you…soon," he said.

I thought for a minute. "Okay, tell her to meet me at the apartment in an hour. I need time to get rid of these guys."

"Okay, I will pass it to her. She did tell me one thing though. Her words were, 'tell him not to do anything stupid.' Now I don't know what she means, but I see trouble on three motorcycles plus I got word that a number of CC Riders are running around in small packs. If I catch you doing something you shouldn't I'll make sure your life becomes very uncomfortable" he said. "Now, get out of my car, I just had it washed."

I got out of the car after he opened the door. As I walked by him I said, "I couldn't have gotten that thing too much dirtier, there was a pig in the front seat." I could almost feel his eyes burning holes in my back.

We got back on the bikes and putted down the road until the cop passed us then we headed for Military. When we got to the dirt road leading to the trailer, I turned in and stopped; the other bikes pulled up on either side of me. "Okay, if I'm right, we will find the place where Casper and his friends are cooking meth. If they're there they will be armed and they will hear us coming. I can only hope they think it's one of their own, but let's just idle in; maybe they won't hear us until we get there."

Both men nodded and we started easing down the road.

It took a few minutes to get near enough to see the trailer. There weren't any bikes there so we pulled up to it and got off. As soon as we walked in the door, I could smell the copper odor of blood. With my .45 in hand I started looking through the trailer. None of the meth equipment was there but the amount of trash and glass jars, along with the ammonia stink of chemicals under the smell of blood, was evidence enough that they had been cooking there.

In the back of the trailer I saw bare feet. I stormed through the trailer and into the room.

Roger was lying in a pool of his own blood. It was evident he had been tortured; there were burns on his feet, chest, arms and face.

Rage exploded through my body and a scream came from somewhere so deep I didn't even recognize it as my own. I looked at my friend's body lying on the floor and I could feel my eyes stinging.

I turned to the other two who had come running. "You pass the word—no one touches a hair on Casper's head. He is mine. As for the other two, their lives are over but if anyone else does anything to any of them, I'll have their asses." I was on the bike in a flash.

I tore off down the dirt road, the big bike barely in control, sliding back and forth but I rolled the throttle hard. When I hit Military I just missed the side of a carload of civilians and rolled past the cage. The driver gave the international signal informing me he was number one...but that was the wrong finger. I headed straight for Dave's, the big bike wide open. I didn't care what was around me. I know I scared the hell out of a few citizens and one state trooper who didn't even see me until I was well past him, the big bike doing over 145.

I rolled into Dave's and went straight to the cooler and got two beers. The first one was down in a flash, the second one half gone before I spoke. "They murdered Roger, Dave. They tortured and murdered him."

"Damn, man, I'm sorry. I didn't really know him but he seemed like a straight-up guy. Who did it, do you know?" he asked.

"Casper and his buddies. Now their asses are mine, all mine."

"Look, TJ, Jean Marie is pretty up front. You need to talk to her," he said.

"No," I said, finishing my beer. "This just became personal. They want to shut down the meth; I'm about to do it for them. They also took out Eddie for some reason, so they all need to die twice." I walked out the door, got on the bike and headed for the apartment.

Jean Marie was already there, sitting in her car. When I pulled up she got out. She followed me to the door. "TJ, we have to talk."

"So, talk, but talk fast. I'm only here for a minute," I told her. "I only stopped because I said I would."

"Okay, TJ, you're off this now. Eddie is dead and the others will be found, so it's over for you," she yelled.

I looked back at her. "Over? Over? No, it just got started. It isn't over until I say it's over. You and our government friends wanted me to do this, so I'm doing it."

She pulled her service revolver. "I'm sorry, TJ, but I have to do what I have to do."

"Jean Marie, they took down Eddie, which is not that big a deal, but they also killed Roger, and for that, they are mine. Now you and I know that you just screwed up; you just played your strongest card and I know you won't use it."

"Where is Roger?" she asked.

"The trailer I told you needed to be checked out. You and your bunch of baby boys in blue have had your chance but you screwed the pooch. Now I'll take care of it," I told her.

"Look, you're part of law enforcement; you can't take this into your own hands."

"Oh, well, I haven't picked up a paycheck in months so I guess quitting shouldn't be a surprise. So, let's make it official, I quit. Now I play this by my rules," I told her as I walked out the door, into the garage and got into the truck.

"TJ, you can't help but go to jail on this. Is that what you want?" she asked.

I laughed. "Yeah, let's see…I shut down the meth lab, the bad guys are put out of commission. Now, I think the good people of Corpus Christi and the great state of Texas will be happy to know they don't have to worry about this bunch selling poison to their kids. Now, I have a criminal to take care of," I said as I rolled out of the drive and headed for the clubhouse.

About half the bikes were back when I arrived. I got out of the truck and walked inside to find Kenny and Red talking to the group. Kenny walked over to me as another group of riders rolled in. "No one could find any of them. Casper isn't at any of his hangouts or his house. Riders have been up and down the beach and saw nothing."

I sat on the pool table trying to think of where they could be. As I sat there members were talking among themselves; one of them came over and said, "Hey, one of the kids that Casper rode with, a kid name Shepherd, has a girlfriend who's a dancer at The Pink Pussycat."

"Does anyone know her name?" Kenny asked.

"I went there and saw her once. She dances as Taffy," one of them said.

I walked to the truck then stopped and turned to a group of riders who had followed me out. "Keep looking for anything and anyone who might give us a lead on Casper and his friends. If you find any of them bring them back here and keep them here. If any of them are unable to talk to me when I get back here I'll stomp the person responsible into the ground. I want Casper; at any cost I want Casper. They had to find someplace else to set up the lab—find out where it is if you can."

The bikers nodded as I climbed into the truck. Kenny crawled into the other side.

"Are you sure you want to be part of this, Kenny? This is your chance to bail before it gets nasty."

"Look, I don't know what, if anything, Casper had to do with the meth business; you are the only one who heard them talking, but I believe you. I do know that Roger was stand-up and I feel pretty confident Casper and his boys had something to do with it. So I'm in this as far as it goes," he said as he closed the door.

I had been to the Pink Pussycat shortly after I got into town. It was a pretty rough little bar and a hangout for some pretty hard core bikers, so in truth I was glad to have Kenny along. I looked in my mirror and there were a dozen bikes behind me. "I guess the club isn't ready to follow my instructions," I said, pointing back toward the bikers.

"I think you're reading that really wrong, bro. I think they're telling you they are behind you as much as I am. Whether you want it or not, with Eddie gone, you are the leader of this club," he said.

"Well, as soon as this thing is over, someone else is going to take the con; that isn't my thing," I told him.

"We'll see, TJ, we'll see," he responded as we pulled into the parking lot of the Pink Pussycat.

We got out as the bikes pulled into the lot. I motioned for them to hold back at the door. Kenny and I walked in, and I almost felt like I was walking into another club's bar. The bartender looked like he ate nails and looked as if he was about to make a grab for me when I asked about Taffy, but I saw his gaze shift toward the door; I turned around to see the bikers strolling inside. Two of them went toward the bathrooms where there was probably another exit. The others took seats around the bar. Now Mr. Nail Eater was looking a little less threatening.

"Taffy is due to be here to go on stage in about an hour—other than that I can't tell you anything," he said.

Kenny went to the other bikers and they soon went back out the door. "I told them to move their bikes just in case our friend shows up."

I turned back to the bartender. "Okay, we'll be waiting outside. If for any reason she doesn't show up you will have a dozen pissed bikers taking this place apart. So I wouldn't suggest that you tell her or her boyfriend we're here."

He was still a tough son of a bitch and I honestly

don't think he was smart enough to be scared. "Look, I have no use for that asshole she is with, so do what you gotta do, but if you touch her I'll be forced to take you down."

I looked at him carefully. "That works for me."

I walked out to the truck and told the rest of the guys to stay out of sight and explained that Kenny and I would be in the truck watching for them. Kenny looked at me. "What are you going to do, TJ?"

I thought for a minute. "One thing at a time—the first thing is to find Casper."

"What are you going to do when you find him?"

"I'm not sure yet, but when I walk away from him he won't be part of depleting the world's supply of oxygen," I told him.

"You can't do that, man! Let's get him and let the courts deal with him."

"Ain't gonna happen. I am going to take great pleasure in taking him down…all the way down. He has violated the law by burning the meth, he has violated biker law by taking down a brother, and he violated my law by taking down a friend. He comes to my court first and in my court there is only one punishment and no appeals," I said angrily as I saw a yellow bike coming up Staples with two riders. It bounced into the lot. Just as she got off the bike, he saw us and headed for the other end of the lot.

Four bikes came ripping around the building and eight more followed quickly. He tried to make it through the parking lot and back to the road. He dumped the clutch, bringing the front wheel three feet off the ground but he couldn't get the front wheel down before he went off the curb and into the street. The bottom of the rear fender hit the curb and sent the bike into a slide. Before he could get up, three men grabbed him and dragged him over to the truck. Two of the men got the bike back on its wheels and pushed it into the lot.

I looked at the man. His left arm was bleeding from contact with the street. "Okay, do you know who I am?" I asked, knowing he did.

He looked at me like he wanted to act all bad-assed but apparently decided that wasn't his best move. "Yeah," he said at last. "You're TJ."

"Okay, so, if you know anything about me you know I am the last person on earth you want pissed at you. I'm going to ask you a few questions and if I like your answers this can end here. If you decide you don't want to be straight with me or I don't like your answer, we're going to the clubhouse to finish this discussion there."

"I'm hurt, man. I need to get to a doc."

I reached out and grabbed the arm and I laughed when he cried out. "Poor baby, three inches of road rash and you act like you're dying. Now, where is Casper?"

"I don't know, he just took off. I haven't seen him today," he said.

"I'm not sure I believe you but I will give you one more chance. Where is Roger?" I asked.

I could see the fear in his eyes now. "Who is Roger?"

He hardly finished saying it before my fist found his face. "Put him in the back of the truck and follow me. Kenny, grab his bike." They found some tie-down straps under the seat and trussed him up like a hog and threw him in the truck. I made sure I took every opportunity to bounce him around as we headed for the meth trailer. When we got there, I jumped out of the truck and dragged him to the ground. Kenny was right behind me and we soon had him inside the trailer. I pointed the way back to where I had found Roger, removed his bonds and pushed him into the corner where Roger had been.

"Okay, I tried to be nice—that shit is over. Since you said you don't know who Roger is I thought maybe you would like to see where I found my friend. Get on your knees," I told him.

He complied then started blubbering, "I didn't do it, man. They sent me out with all the stuff. I never touched him, I swear."

My foot found his chest and he bounced off the wall. "It's not that I don't believe you. I just don't like your answer. Now, would you like to guess what happens if I don't believe you? Let's try this again, where is Casper?"

Two of the men dragged him back to his knees. "I honestly don't know. He took the stuff and disappeared. He took the cash, the stuff, everything."

"Okay, for now let's say I believe you. Who is the other member of your team and where can I find him? Before you answer let me tell you something. First, my friend is dead; second the president of the club was murdered and a lot of brothers want you guys for that. So, while I am asking you specific questions you better tell me the whole deal or I turn you over to the club—and they aren't as nice as I am."

"The other guy's name is Bryan. He lives with some other guy, an old guy out on Padre Island. Okay, the whole story is that Casper knew we were running to Mexico and running stuff back across the border. He asked us if we wanted to make real money and we jumped on it. Casper got Eddie involved but I don't know how much he knew. Both Casper and

Bryan are crazy. Casper started using the stuff and went off the deep end. What else do you want to know?" he asked.

"Who did Eddie?" I asked.

"Casper said Eddie was asking for a bigger cut and after Casper got booted out of the club he said he was going to get Eddie," he said.

"You guys couldn't have gotten away with this for so long if you hadn't had help from the cops. Who was the contact?" I asked.

"You're right, but I don't know who it was. I'm pretty sure that was all Eddie. That's why he was getting a fifty percent cut," he said.

"Is that why Eddie was taken out?" I asked.

"I didn't even know that happened. I haven't seen anyone 'cept Bryan since we tore down the lab and he didn't say anything about Eddie," he lied.

The toe of my boot caught him in the ribs. "We're through. You just lied to me. I saw Eddie's, Bryan's, Casper's and your bikes at the clubhouse just before Eddie was murdered. I think you just signed your death warrant."

I heard a female voice behind me. "No, TJ, he is mine and I am taking him downtown."

"Not this time, Jean Marie. This punk has been involved in the murder of two people and he has to stand in my court first. If there is anything left you can have him."

"TJ, this is a mistake, you know that. Are you going to be the same kind of animal this guy is?" she asked.

"No, this animal is a cowardly mutt. I am simply going to show him who the alpha male is. Now, get out of here before you get your hands dirty and yourself in trouble. Right now you don't know anything—keep it that way." I saw her hand slip toward her revolver. "Don't do that," I told her. "For one, you won't use it and secondly you will just embarrass yourself."

"TJ, this is a big mistake," she said again.

If I hadn't had a dozen bikers around me I might have been able to back down and let her have this pitiful excuse for human flesh but to back down would turn this whole group on me. I turned to Kenny as Jean Marie walked out. "Take this mutt to the clubhouse and grab your bike, then come to the apartment. I'll take his bike. Tell everyone at the club that if anything happens to this piece of crap before I get back they will answer to me." I turned to the rest of the guys standing there. "There are two more people to find. I'm going after Casper. The rest of you see if you can find Bryan and take him to the clubhouse…and I want him whole and breathing."

Jean Marie was getting into her car when I stepped out. "Jean, I can't turn this guy over to you with the club standing there. I promise I will try to keep him alive but for now I need to make sure he can't get to anyone."

She looked at me angrily. "How the hell do you think he is going to get to anyone if I have him? Are you starting to doubt me too?"

I shook my head. "Nope, I trust you but there is someone in the department who is clearing the way for these guys. If that person finds out then two things are going to happen: our little boy in there is going to let it all out and he is going to be dead. At least my guys will make sure he is kept out of sight and he has the best chance of being alive when this is over."

"Those guys in there will kill him. One way or another they will kill him," she said.

"No, that won't happen. My guys are true to the club if nothing else, and for the time being I am the top of that club. Now, if you really want to be helpful find out what vehicles William Carr owns and get that information to the State Police and the border at Nuevo Laredo. He could already be there but if he isn't maybe they can snag him with drugs and weapons. On the way back he will still be carrying," I told her.

"I'm going to play this your way, TJ, not because I particularly want to but because you have been right too many times to just walk away from it. But if anything happens to him, I won't be able to cover your ass," she warned.

"Don't worry. If anything happens to him, you won't ever see him again. There are seventy guys in the club who will happily turn him into smoke just for what he did to Eddie. Now, I am going to the apartment and make some calls. I need some help you can't give," I explained as I stepped across the gaudy chopper and turned it toward the house.

As soon as I got home, I called Jimmy and once again his sweet sounding wife answered. When I asked for him she said hesitantly, "Okay, TJ, but I am going to warn you right now. I hear trouble in your voice and if anything happens to my husband I will hunt you down."

"What's up, Lil Brother?" he asked. I had almost forgotten that nickname. I don't know what started it but some of the guys started calling me that and it soon became my name around the club.

"Jimmy, I need your help bad but after hearing your wife's warning I'm not so sure," I told him.

"She's pregnant, bro. They get that way sometimes. What do you need?"

I thought for a minute. I didn't want to see another friend hurt but maybe he could help in another way. "I need to get across the border without any hassle. Can you help me?"

"Why would you be hassled, man? You gonna be carrying something the man may not like?" Curiosity filled his voice.

"Yes, but it isn't drugs. I'm pretty sure Casper has already made it across the border and is probably holed up in Boy's Town. I don't know whether he has sold the meth or not," I said then thought of something. "If he was going to unload it to another club, who would that be?"

He was silent for a time. "There is a club down that way called Dark Soldiers. It is made up of a bunch of misfits and wannabes. They would be my best guess."

"Do you have any names for me?" I asked.

"No, but I can get the leader's name pretty quick. I know they hang in a bar named McGill's on the south side of Laredo and at the ABC Bar in Boy's Town," he told me.

"Okay, get me what you can and I will do some more digging. I will be here for a little while longer. If you find something call me."

"I'm going, bro. My chopper is drawing cobwebs and I am itching to blow the dust off," he said.

"No way, Jimmy, you have too much to lose. Kenny and I are pretty much solo. If this goes bad no one will be losing a husband or father. You stay at home where you belong," I told him.

"Sorry, bro, I will be on the highway waiting. You try to blow me off and I will have you stopped long before you make it to Laredo." I heard a strength I didn't remember in his voice. "Besides, Sandy is still intent on talking to you and if anything happens to you I will have to move out of the state," he said laughing.

"Okay, bro, but you are riding with two club members. You do exactly what I tell you. I will not tell your wife I was the cause of you getting hurt. Got it?" I asked.

"Got it, let's roll," he said.

I told him when I thought we would be down his way and he told me where he would be. Next I called information for Laredo to find McGill's. It was easier than I thought and I placed the call.

When the gruff voice picked up the phone I explained I was president of the CC Riders club and was looking for the president of Dark Soldiers. In a few minutes a clearly Mexican voice came on the line. "Eddie, been a while, bro."

"This isn't Eddie; he died this morning," I told him.

"Can't be true, man. What happened, and who are you?" he asked.

I hesitated. "I am on my way down there and would rather explain it all in person. It's a pretty bad situation. As for me, just call me Lil Brother. I'm one of the original members of the club," I explained.

"Hey, I know you, man. You joined the Navy, right?" he asked.

"That's right but some other things are happening now. Have you seen Casper?" I asked.

"He's here now," then silence, "at least he was when I came to the phone." He yelled at someone then came back to the phone. "He split, man, right after Richie told me who was on the line. You want me to find him?"

I thought about it. "No, I'll be down there as

quickly as I can. Keep your people there until I get there. I may need some help."

"Did that little bastard do Eddie? I'll kill the—"

I interrupted. "I need you to keep cool with this. I really need to find him and talk to him. Please, bro, don't go after him," I begged.

"I have to trust you know what you're doing. Okay, bro, we will be here, but hurry before we get too drunk," he laughed then told me how to find the bar.

I grabbed my pack and threw in a few things including more guns and ammunition than I hoped I needed then grabbed the three thousand and stuffed it in my pockets. I heard Kenny's bike roll into the yard.

CHAPTER FIFTEEN

Kenny and I loaded our stuff on the bikes without much discussion. When I asked if he was carrying he nodded in the affirmative. "Put it in my bag; there is less chance they will search us all and I think I will be clear," I said explaining about Jimmy. I went back into the apartment and found one of my cutoffs and stuck it in my bag. Just as we pulled out of the garage Jean Marie and Sherry pulled up.

They got out of the car and walked over to me; Sherry spoke first. "TJ, stop, right now. I lost a good friend in Roger. I'll be damned if I lose another one."

I put my hands on her shoulders. "I will be fine; it's Casper who needs someone's concern." I looked at Jean Marie. "I will try to bring him back, I promise, but there is a whole group of bikers down there who want him too."

There were tears in Sherry's eyes. "Look, Roger meant for you and me to stay friends. He left us both a nice lump but unless you become my partner in the bar we get none of it."

"All the more reason for me to make sure I make it back and to put an end to Casper and his little friends; that way we can just rock on with our lives. Gee, me a bar owner, never thought I would ever own a bar," I said.

She slapped my left shoulder. "It is still my bar; you are a silent partner, very silent. Oh, and someone named Sandy has been calling for you. Is that who I think it is?" she asked.

I smiled. "Yeah, if she calls again tell her I will be in touch after her brother and I get back from Mexico. Now, we gotta get out of here; we have someone waiting." I stepped across the bike, fired it up and kicked it in gear. Sherry ran to the bike and I could barely hear her tell me to be careful above the rumble of the engine.

I rolled the throttle hard when we hit the street and headed for the high rise. Coming down the high rise I saw a state trooper pull onto the road and allowed us to catch him. When we got next to him he waved for us to follow him. In a matter of a few seconds he had the Oldsmobile rolling at one-thirty, lights and siren going. I had never had a cop in front of me with his lights on—they were usually behind me.

The trip to meet Jimmy took less than half the time it usually would and there was another car waiting with Jimmy. The 145-mile trip took us a little over an hour. I had never driven that fast for that long; maybe I should have become a cop. When we got to the edge of town we were met by locals who asked where we needed to go. When we told them where and gave them a short why, they looked at each other a little strange and took us right up to McGill's.

As we got off the bikes I grabbed my bag, opened it, grabbed my old vest and threw it to Jimmy. "We are flying colors—you just became a member pro-temp." He put on the vest, which was a little short for him, but his swagger told me he never really left the club.

We were greeted by the biggest, ugliest, meanest looking Mexican I have ever seen in my life who looked at our colors and I thought for a minute we had made a mistake wearing them. He handed each of us a beer as we walked through the door and pointed us to a large table where a half-dozen bikers sat. As we walked to the table the second biggest Mexican I have ever seen stood up and came to me with open arms and welcomed us.

Everyone but the big guy left the table. "I am Julio, they call me Cuchillo Loco. Sounds more like an Indian name—it means Crazy Knife." With that he pulled a ripple-edged knife from the sheath on his belt; the blade was easily twelve inches long. "Just call me Julio," he said as he put the knife away.

We made introductions all around. I even explained that Jimmy was a state cop, which Julio thought was funny. He laughed, "Damn, never thought about getting a cop in the club, shit, damned good idea." He leaned in. "Okay, now tell me about Eddie. We were pretty close."

I explained about the meth and the part Eddie played in it and about what happened to him. "I need to find Casper; he owes the club for taking Eddie out."

There was a fiery rage in his eyes. "Leave him to us—that mother gonna take a long time to die."

Now I had to be a little cautious. I didn't want to insult him. "Julio, this is club business. The club has a right to see this thing to the end. While I appreciate how you are hurt by this, my guys would be very upset with me if I allowed anyone else to take retribution. You understand; if the shoe was on the other foot I would respect your position."

He sat there fuming; I just prayed he wasn't fuming about me. "Not many people would come into my town and say this to me. This maricon has killed my friend. I can't let it go. But you too have your right to him and are responsible to the club to bring him back. We will do whatever you need."

I considered his offer for a moment. "I need Casper in one piece, but how do I find him and how do I get him back across the border?"

Julio looked at me like I was some kind of nut. "Tell you what, gringo. You go across and into Boy's Town. The ABC Bar is in the middle of the third block, and there is a kid who will offer to watch your bikes; give him five bucks apiece. Don't give him any more than that or he will jack up the price and I will have to kick his butt. Wait there for us."

"Okay, we don't have any choice but to trust you. Just get him to us so we can get him back to Corpus," I told him.

"You got it, bro," he said as he turned toward the door.

"Julio," I said, causing the big man to stop, "what was your business with Eddie and Casper?"

He looked at me then at Jimmy. "Eddie introduced me to Casper, said Casper had some primo meth to turn over for a decent price. Eddie never seemed completely comfortable with it and was never around when a deal went down."

"Did Casper bring any this time?" I asked.

"I bought about five grand's worth. He delivered but I haven't paid him yet." He smiled. "I just might not have to."

"That's between you two, I just need him," I said and walked toward the door.

"Ok, bro. You guys head to the bar. I'll see you in a bit," he said as he walked toward a gaudy custom Harley trike.

We rode across the border with the cops there eyeing us then headed for Boy's Town and found the bar with ease. Sure enough when we pulled up a ten-year-old boy came over. "Watch your bikes? No one touch, they safe with me," he said lifting his shirt to show a pistol tucked in his waistband.

I couldn't tell whether it was real or not, but I had to give the kid credit either way. I pulled out a five. "Five dollars, you watch all three," I said.

"You crazy, gringo—five each," he said.

"Ten, all three," I said pulling out another five.

He thought for a minute. "Okay, you pay now," he said.

I took the two fives, tore them in half handing him two halves and sticking the other two in my pocket. "You get the rest when we come out, maybe more."

He took the two halves of the bills and just shook his head as he stuck them in his pocket. "Loco gringo."

The bar was a dump by any standard. I was no prude and I certainly didn't hang out in high society pubs, but this was bad. The floors were so filthy I couldn't tell whether there was any wood down there or not. Two half-dressed women smiled at us expectantly, displaying mouths only half filled with yellow teeth. I looked at the hag behind the bar. "Dos Equis," I said as I walked to a table near the back but where we could see the bikes through the filthy window. The lumbering old bag brought three beers and three filthy glasses; I gave her the money for the beer and handed her the glasses back. The beer was not as cold as I would have liked but it was as cold as I expected.

We sat in that rat hole for two hours then Kenny looked at me. "I think we have been had, man."

I agreed with him. "I think our new friends have

crossed us; let's go back across the river before we find ourselves in trouble."

When we walked out, the kid pointed the gun at us. "Now gimme your money," he said seriously.

I reached for the two half fives in my shirt then pulled a twenty from my wallet; as he reached for it I snatched the old revolver from his hand and pushed him to the ground. I looked at his now tear-streaked filthy face. "That twenty was going to be yours," I threw the two half bills at him, "now you can take your few pennies and your scrawny ass and get out of here."

"Give me my gun!" he screamed.

I threw the old gun as far as I could; it landed in a filthy ditch. "Go get it, boy," I laughed. I was pissed and the boy had just pushed the wrong button. I sat there with the bike idling for a minute then motioned the boy over again; warily he came over. I reached into my pocket and pulled out the twenty. "Do you know Cuchillo Loco?" I asked.

He looked at the bill and shook his head. I pulled another one out and I could see sadness in his eyes— evidently he honestly didn't and yet he didn't want to tell me that. I handed him the money and held out my hand to shake his.

"Gracias, mucho gracias. I watch your bikes for free, any time."

We headed down the dirt road then back on the main road to the border. When we got there we were motioned to the side and three of Mexico's finest held us at gunpoint as a sweaty cop came over. He looked at the bag on the back of my bike. "Do you have anything to declare? What is in the bag?" he asked.

So, Julio had set us up.

Before I could answer Jimmy stepped off his bike and, ignoring the sound of pistols being cocked, reached into his pocket and brought out his badge and identification. He pushed them into the man's face and began talking to him in rapid fire Spanish. The color drained from the man's face as he motioned for his men to put their arms away. The two men talked more quietly for a few minutes more then Jimmy walked back to his bike.

As he was putting on his gloves he said, "Julio and his boys including the pearl white bike came through here about an hour ago."

"Okay, that means he has the group behind him. Let's go back to their little hangout and see what we find."

We took off to the bar. I had no idea where we were going from there. When we got to the bar there were at least thirty bikes there including Casper's. We stopped just out of sight from the bar on a little rise of land and looked down at the place.

Kenny shook his head. "TJ, this doesn't look like the kind of odds I like," he said as he checked the loads in his gun.

"I don't either, but we can't just walk away—if we don't leave some kind of mark we will never be able to hold our heads up," I said looking down at the building. "Jimmy, swing around to the back. I know we aren't going to walk out of here with Casper but we have to do something. I will give you time to get to that back door. Kenny, walk in with me; be ready for anything."

Jimmy got off his bike and pushed it around the outside of the parking lot, setting it up pointing away for a fast escape. When I saw him disappear around the building, Kenny and I rode in and parked the bikes pointing toward the road then stepped off and headed for the door.

The same huge Mexican was standing at the door blocking it as we walked up the steps. He started reaching for something in his waistband. I stepped forward quickly with my .45 and shoved it hard against his ear. I found the .44 magnum stuffed in his pants and the large knife hanging on his side. I took them both and pushed him ahead of me. Another rider came out with a knife. Kenny took out first one kneecap and then the other and removed the knife and two automatics from his belt. I pointed my .45 at the bartender and motioned him around the bar then went behind the bar so no one could slip behind me.

I looked over at Julio and Casper. "Let's go, Casper. You have to answer to the club for what happened to Eddie."

Julio spoke up before Casper could answer. "Sorry about that, TJ. I can't allow another club to take a patch holder." He saw the confusion on my face and laughed. "Sorry, man, I guess there is no way for you to know that he has been wearing our patch for almost two years."

"He still has to answer to the club. I don't give a damn whose patch he wears. He took down one of ours and he will answer for it. If you insist on protecting him I'm going to have a hundred riders here taking you and your little band down. In the end we will get him."

Julio smiled. "I see two gringos standing in my bar, in my town telling me what I am going to do. What makes you think you will even walk out of here?"

I kept my eyes on Julio. "Jimmy, if anyone even looks like they want to move put your first round in our fat Mexican friend's head."

"No sweat, TJ. I couldn't miss that piece of shit if I tried," he said then put a round into the table leg causing the table to fall to the floor. Julio had a large revolver sitting in his lap.

"Julio, pick that cannon up by the barrel and drop it on the floor!" I yelled at the Mexican. The big guy who had been at the door charged around the bar. I put a .45 round in his leg just above the knee. He fell to the floor. "Damn it, Jimmy! I told you to shoot that fat bastard if anyone moved," I yelled.

He laughed. "I figured you wanted to have a little fun. I won't hesitate next time."

I looked at Julio. "Okay, let's call this one a standoff, but we will be back with enough riders to take over this town. Casper, you better make your peace because you're a dead man."

Casper laughed and looked around. "These are my new friends, TJ. I make what they need. You think they are going to let me go? No way, man. Besides the fact that you are no one to the club, they won't follow you. I will be back in Corpus and the club will be mine."

I wanted to put a round right between his eyes, but the club deserved the opportunity to make the call on him. I looked directly at Casper. "You called this one wrong, Casper. You put Eddie down. It doesn't matter who is at the top of the club, you will go down. We are coming back and when we do, you will be going back to Corpus."

I looked around the room—we had pressed our luck too far as it was. I looked back at Julio. "We're leaving, but we will be back. In the meantime you better think about whether you want to risk your club by holding onto him. If anyone comes out of this bar before we hit the road we will start blowing holes in Harleys. Jimmy, start your bike then come around front. When we come out feel free to drop anyone behind us."

Jimmy went out and lit off his Harley while I made sure no one moved. As soon as he was at the front I sent Kenny out then to start our bikes then turned back to Julio. "Don't back this horse, Julio; we will be back and we will get him and we will not hesitate to put anyone down who gets in our way." I backed to the door and turned loose four rounds into the ceiling then ran for my bike and we rolled hard out of the parking lot.

We tube locked the throttles and headed out of town. I knew my machine was fast enough to blow them off if they did come after us but Kenny and Jimmy couldn't keep up. As we hit a hard curve leaving town I saw the cut off to an old road and made a run for it. When we were far enough to be out of sight we pulled over and turned the bikes off. I got off my bike and sat under a tree, shaking like crazy.

Kenny came over and handed me a cigarette. I took it and took a long drag trying to calm my nerves. "What now, TJ? They are going to be waiting for us..." The roar of bikes on the main road sounded like thunder as they blew past.

We sat there for a couple of hours, all of us quiet. We had just come very close to being very dead and now we had thirty riders looking for us. The bikes were coming back; we sat there hoping they had given up, not that they had figured out what we did. Soon they passed by and we went to our bikes.

I looked at the two of them. "Okay, let's head back but watch and be ready. They could have left riders along the road. I have a plan boiling. Let's get back to the clubhouse. Kenny, as soon as we hit North Beach I want you to stop and call the clubhouse and have them round up every rider they can, I don't care whether they are member, prospects or friends. Round up everyone possible. Jimmy, you go straight to the clubhouse and start getting everyone ready and gassed up. I will meet you at the clubhouse as soon as I can."

We got on the road and headed for home. Surprisingly, there was no one waiting for us along the road. As soon as we hit town Kenny peeled off to make the calls. A little further along I motioned for Jimmy to head for the clubhouse and I turned toward the Blue Note.

I pulled around behind the bar and went inside to find Sherry. She was in her office; when I opened the door she ran up and threw her arms around me.

"Did you find Casper?" she asked.

"I'll tell you in a few minutes but first I need you to get in touch with Jean Marie and get her out here fast. I don't have much time so get her here right away."

Sherry got on the phone and finally found Jean Marie who promised to get to the bar in the next twenty minutes. After she got off the phone I told Sherry the entire story and when Jean Marie arrived I repeated it.

Jean Marie sat there shaking her head. "So why have you called me?"

"Jean Marie, I am going to get Casper and bring him back to stand in front of the club. After they have passed judgment and the sentence has been carried out I will turn myself in. I am asking you to turn your back long enough to get that done," I told her.

"TJ, you are going to end up with your ass in jail for a hell of a long time. I'm not turning my back or I would be right there with you so you can forget that," she answered.

I was getting a little ticked at her now. "Look, you, the Navy and the government got me into this thing to shut down the meth operation; you were part of talking me into involving other people in this mess and because of that Roger is dead. If you think I'm going to allow that son of a bitch to walk away you're nuts!"

"We will get him, we will bring him in, and he will stand trial," she snarled. "You're not a cop, you're not a judge," her eyes almost spitting fire.

"It's a damned good thing I'm not! The police couldn't even shut down the meth operation, couldn't even get it right as to who was doing what and you expect me to believe that now you will catch Casper and make sure he goes to jail? Get serious! Your whole damned police department is made up of a bunch of misfits who couldn't put their pants on right without outside training. No! I am bringing down Casper. I am going to see he pays for what he has done. Be smart, because friend or no friend, if you get in my way I will put you down too," I screamed then started for the door.

"Why did you call me here if you aren't going to listen to me, damn it?" she yelled at my back.

I stopped, turned around and looked at her. "Because I thought you would want to do the right thing, because I thought Roger was your friend too, because I thought you were my friend, and because I thought you would understand. Unfortunately none of that is true; you are just another brainwashed city employee. So, do what you do best—go back to your office and take a nap while I do your work for you." I turned and stormed out the door before she could respond.

I got on the bike and tore out for the clubhouse. I was tearing up ground when I saw a bunch of bikes running up toward me. I was pretty sure I could outrun them and get to the clubhouse well ahead of them, but I wasn't sure who would be there. I knew there was a crossover coming up so I backed off and allowed the riders to catch up a little. There were four of them. I allowed them to get right on my tail then laid the big bike over and hit the crossover.

As I had hoped, they overshot it. I grabbed the throttle and twisted hard, screaming through the gears until I hit the first curve then dropped into a neighborhood and waited for them to pass. Once they did I turned back toward the clubhouse and ran hard.

When I got there, the parking lot was full. Shepherd and Bryan, the two bikers who had worked with Casper, were inside tied to chairs. I walked in, looked at them then at the hundred-plus bikers filling the room. It was time to make some serious decisions.

CHAPTER SIXTEEN

The clubhouse was packed to the walls and so noisy I couldn't even think. I walked across the room to where the two men were secured to chairs and the room gradually got stone quiet. I jumped up on another chair and looked around the room. "We have a problem. In fact we have more than one and we need to figure out how to deal with them. First, and to me the least, is the issue of these two rats."

The room suddenly got loud with everyone yelling at once. I raised my hands and asked for quiet again. Once things settled down I started again. "Before we deal with that let me make things a little clearer about where I am coming from. Many of you may not know me—my name is TJ and I am one of the original members of this club; in fact I am one of the only remaining original members. The other two are Casper and Kenny. Kenny was the twelfth member and until we change the rules the leadership of this club falls to me, at least until or if I pass that to someone else."

The room was pretty quiet when one of the members asked, "So, you are taking the lead. I can go with that, that's fine, but what do we do with these two?"

A lot of suggestions were made, none of which would result in them seeing daylight again and most were more than a little painful. I asked Kenny to step up on the table and asked for quiet again. "Look, other than the fact that they ran with Casper, there is nothing to indicate these two have done anything wrong that we are concerned with. They were cooking meth and causing some trouble for some friends of mine, but that is a matter for the police."

There was a rumble through the clubhouse. Another member stepped up. "Okay, you are the president of this club, what you decide is what we will do." He turned to the rest of the members. "This is not a democracy. You joined this club knowing what the rules are. Whether we agree or not, as long as we are members we will back the president." He turned back to me. "TJ, I'm Snake, and I am behind you one hundred percent."

I looked over the rest of the club. "Anyone who isn't with me, drop your colors on your way out the door. There won't be any hard feelings, just don't come back around." The room was deathly quiet and no one moved. "Okay, I take it we are all on the same page. For the next hour I want this clubhouse empty except for these two little boys over here, Kenny, Snake, Jimmy and me. Find any riders who are ready and willing for a fight and we will meet at Bob Hall Pier in an hour. Now go!"

As the clubhouse was emptying and the bikes were roaring out of the lot I walked to the office and dialed Jean Marie's number. When she answered I spoke quietly. "Jean Marie, I have the two boys who rode with Casper and were cooking meth with him. They were also involved in killing Roger and I would love nothing more than to cut them to pieces but I am going to turn them over to you."

She was quiet for a minute. "What about Casper?"

"I don't have him yet, and I won't make any

promises when I do find him, but if you get someone out here you can have these two. If you don't want them, we will be happy to take care of them for you."

"I'm on my way. Can I bring another officer with me?" she asked.

"Of course, but please make sure it is someone trustworthy," I said and hung up the phone.

I walked back inside the main room and called Kenny and Snake over out of earshot of Casper's friends. "Okay, Snake, you are now the Road Captain, and Kenny, you are vice. I will announce all this before we make our ride."

Snake beamed but Kenny looked a little unsure. "TJ, I don't know that this club has ever had a vice. Look, man, I'm just a member, nothing more."

"Kenny, we don't have time for a long, drawn out discussion about this thing. You are the vice and if anything happens to me you have the club. Now, down to business. Who has a van we can get our hands on for a few hours?" I asked.

Snake said, "My boss has an old beat up panel van. It runs good, it's just ugly as hell."

"I knew there was a reason I wanted you here. Okay, if you can get it, let's get it here and gassed up," I said.

Snake went into the office and used the phone. "Kenny, I am going with Snake. You take the rest of the club and break them into smaller groups then meet up on the other side of Freer; we don't want to get too close. I will explain everything then. Grab the CB radios out of the office and bring me the car mount."

Snake came back into the room. "We have the van. Do I need to pick up anything else while I'm out?"

I thought for a minute. "Do you have a gun?"

"Never cared much for guns," he said as he reached down to his left boot and removed a large bowie-style knife and deftly threw it across the room and buried it in the dart board just off center. He shook his head angrily. "I must be getting rusty."

"Okay, then, just make sure the van is gassed up and ready to go," I told him.

He walked over to the board, removed the knife and dropped it in his boot. "Okay, seeya in about thirty minutes," and walked out of the room.

Kenny brought the radio to me. "I don't know what you have in mind, but I sure hope you know what you're doing," he said as he was leaving.

"So do I," Jimmy said.

"Jimmy, I want you to take my pickup out there and head for Laredo. I need you to find out where Casper is holed up," I said handing him the keys, "then meet us near Freer."

"Do you want me to do anything if I find him?" he asked.

"Not a thing except get back to us pronto."

"What the hell do you have in mind, TJ?"

"Okay, here it is. I want to find him away from the bar. The club will ride in after we get to where he is and while Julio is trying to figure out what to do with a hundred bikers we will snag Casper and get him out of town," I explained.

"Then what?" he asked.

"Then you will go home to your wife and pretend we haven't seen each other in years. Now go!" I said as I saw the police cruiser pull into the parking lot.

Jean Marie came in along with a very large cop. "I take it these are the two. Have they admitted anything?"

"Not to me, but if they won't admit it to you then just leave them here and the club will hold court and question them," I told her.

"Don't leave us here," one of them said near tears. "This room was full of bikers that wanted to take us out and drag us down the road,"

Jean Marie walked over to them. "Right now, I really don't have anything to arrest you boys for. I mean TJ has said you killed his friend and were involved with cooking and selling meth and while that would be more than sufficient in this biker court, it isn't even enough to do more than question you."

I looked at the two men then back at Jean Marie. "If these two hit the streets again I won't call you next time. We'll take care of it ourselves."

One of the men spoke up. "We sold the meth and helped Casper cook it up. Can't say anything about anybody getting killed."

She looked at her partner. "Sounds like a confession to the manufacture and distribution of methamphetamines; read them their rights then see if they want to repeat their story."

Her partner read them their rights and they quickly told the story again. Jean Marie nodded toward the office. "Let's talk before I go."

We went into the office and I sat on the edge of the desk. "No more lectures. I know what I am doing isn't legal but you guys can't burn this turkey legally," I told her.

"I know, TJ, I know. I am going to say this and if anyone ever asks me I will swear on my living mother's grave I never said it. You get Casper, but if you do him, don't leave any way to be caught. It doesn't matter if everyone in the world is certain you did it if there is no way to tie it to you. Now, officially, I am telling you to let the law deal with him." She kissed me on the cheek. "Be careful," she whispered then walked out the door.

I sat back on the pool table, alone in the quiet room. It was the first time in what seemed like forever that I could be alone with my thoughts. I was upset about Eddie, even though he was doing things in the club that weren't right, but that wasn't any reason to want him dead. Mostly I was pissed about Roger; he hadn't done a damned thing to anyone and they killed him. Was I going about this the right way? Was there another way that made sense to me? Yeah, I knew the law had a right to have their opportunity to take care of this but they had failed in the past. No, I had to do it this way, no matter what the cost. I knew I would never be the same person after this, after today.

I began mulling over my issues with the Navy and this mess. My enlistment had expired; of course my government friends had promised they would take care of it but they were the ones who got me here to start with. Where was my life going from here, from tomorrow, because my life would start over when this was finished. I thought about Sandy—what was she going to think about all of this, or did it really matter?

I heard a vehicle pulling into the drive and went to the door. Snake was just stepping out of an old work van that must have been red at one time. He walked toward me. "It looks like shit but it runs like hell. What now, TJ?"

"I need to go by my place and pick up some things and drop off my bike. Follow me over there," I said as I stepped across the Harley, fired it up and pulled from the parking lot.

When we pulled up at the apartment I motioned for Snake to follow me inside.

"Nice digs," he said.

"The place belonged to a friend who recently died, not sure how much longer I will be here," I said as I walked into the house. I grabbed a couple of my bags and began loading a couple of .45s, a long gun and a couple of shotguns inside plus all the ammunition I could find. Then I grabbed a couple of sleeping bags, blankets and some rope. The nights tend to chill this time of year, and I wasn't sure how long we would be. I was about to walk out the door when I thought about Sherry. I handed everything to Snake. "I will be out in a few minutes. I need to make a call before we get out of here."

Sherry picked up on the second ring. "Hey Sherry, I wanted to touch base before I get out of here," I told her.

Her voice sounded choked. "Where the hell are you going, TJ? I talked to Jean Marie a little while ago. She has two of the men. What are you going to do?"

"She doesn't have Casper. He is in Laredo and we are going down there to get him," I told her.

"Who is we?" she asked.

"The club is going down, just to make sure we don't have any problems."

"Now I am concerned. You are taking a hundred bikers to Laredo to retrieve one person? That seems a little excessive," she said.

I was giving her too much information. "Look, it is club business and the club needs to take care of it as a group."

"Is that another way of saying there are a bunch

of thugs down there you expect to have trouble with?" she asked.

"Everything is fine. I gotta get out of here and get on the road. I will see you when I get back."

"You better get your ass back here. I lost a friend in Roger. I don't plan to bury two friends in the same year."

"Look, I will be fine, I will be back—after all I don't even have a will. Bye," I said as I hung up the phone and ran to the van before she could call back. I got in and looked at Snake. "Okay, let's go south. Don't get in too big a hurry. I want everyone to beat us down there."

Once we hit the highway Snake looked at me. "I remember you from before you went in the Navy. Now I see you back here and I hear you aren't in the Navy any more. What's the story?"

"It's a very long story but let me see if I can shrink it into a short lump. I got tired of the way things were around here and decided I needed to get away so I chose the Navy. It was safe enough; I mean who shoots at big ships? One day they were looking for volunteers for river patrol so Mike Kaufman and I volunteered," I stopped for a minute to get a drink.

"I remember Mike; he came to the club just before I did. I think I remember the two of you joining together," he said.

"Yeah, Mike and I went in under the 'Buddy Plan,' which meant we would be stationed together, at least until he blew the psych exam. Can you imagine being unfit psychologically to kill people? Anyway, they took me, sent me through some…uh…special training then dropped me on a patrol boat as a gunner. I stayed on that boat for two tours because I was too stupid to leave," I laughed.

He laughed along with me. "Then what?"

"Well, I was sent to an attack squadron assigned to a place in the California desert. After that tour was complete I asked for hometown duty and got it. Then came the real fun, I got into trouble and here I am," I told him.

We talked for a bit longer then I kicked back in the uncomfortable seat and dozed off until a bunch of static and squawking from the CB radio woke me. I listened but I couldn't understand a word. We were just pulling into Freer so I just sat back and waited until we got back on the highway. A local cop gave us a curious glance but didn't really pay much attention fortunately—having some redneck cop stopping us right now wouldn't be fun. I wondered whether he had seen the bikers coming through.

The static on the channel we had selected continued as we drove out of town. With Freer and their little town cop behind us I felt a little better. After a few minutes we could hear Kenny trying to get through with the little hand-held unit. I squawked back that he was coming through weak and that we would try them in a few minutes. After another fifteen minutes Kenny was coming in clear and he tried to explain where they were. I told him to send one bike to the highway to lead us to them. A little while later I saw a single rider sitting on the side of the road and we pulled up behind him.

I got out of the van and walked to the rider. "How far away?" I asked.

"Just a couple of miles," he said as he stepped across the full-dressed Harley.

We followed him up the road a ways then turned onto a paved side road. Two hundred yards later we pulled into a clearing where over one hundred bikers sat impatiently.

Kenny walked over. "Hey, bro, we were beginning to think you got lost," he said as we clasped hands. "What's the plan?"

"Have you heard anything from Jimmy?" I asked.

"Yeah, he cruised the bar but didn't see Casper's bike. Then he stopped a couple of places but hasn't had any luck finding him," he replied.

I told Kenny and Snake to come over next to the van. I looked at the two men. "Okay, it looks like we are going to have to go into the bar, but I don't want to take everyone in at one time. Find me fifteen or twenty riders whose bikes aren't too loud then bring them over," I told Kenny.

In a few minutes he returned with about twenty-five riders. "Quietest of the bunch. What do you have in mind, bro?"

I looked around at the crew—most of them were weathered riders, men as hard as they come and chomping at the bit to get moving on something. "Okay, Kenny, listen close because I only want to take time to tell this once. You guys," I said to the riders, "are going to follow us into town. The bar is down below a small hill. You guys are going to pull into cover before we get there. Two other riders on loud bikes will follow us down to the bar."

Kenny called two others over to listen.

I looked at the two. "You guys follow us into the parking lot of the bar. Keep your bikes in lower gears so we can hide the sound of the other bikes. If something starts going down, the bikers waiting up the hill come storming into the parking lot, and be ready for anything." I looked back at Kenny. "Give us a twenty-minute head start then come on in, ride straight into the parking lot in force. Again, be ready for anything. If the other riders are already in the parking lot take for granted there is some trouble. Be ready," I told them.

Everyone seemed to understand so we mounted up, the two loud choppers behind us and the other bikes behind them. When we got to the hill I motioned for the two riders to follow us and the other bikers to peel off. We drove into the parking lot and watched as the big Mexican opened the door then went back inside. There were at least forty bikes in the parking lot.

CHAPTER SEVENTEEN

As we rolled up to the front door, Julio stood in the doorway along with the big guy just as we rolled to a stop. I stepped out of the van and stood next to the right front wheel, my .45 tucked loosely in my belt. Julio looked at the two riders and Snake. "I know you didn't come here to cause any trouble, not with only four of you," Julio said.

I leaned against the truck. "Not here for any trouble. We are just here to take Casper back so the club can decide what to do with him."

Julio looked around, almost as though he were sniffing the air for trouble. "TJ, I don't know you very well, not at all really, but I never thought of you as a man who would ride into an armed camp unless it was your own or you had the advantage. I don't see that as being true in either case."

I looked around and could see a couple of heads sticking out from the far corner of the building. One of the riders saw it and turned to stare directly at the faces. "I don't know you very well either, Julio, but I can't imagine you would cross another club and protect a member who has crossed his own people. I never figured you as someone who would hide a coward," I said.

His eyes hardened. "Are you calling me a coward?" he asked.

I rested my right hand on my hip, just a few inches from the butt of the automatic. "I never said anything of the kind, no; if I called you a coward I would have simply said you were a chicken shit spic bastard and I don't remember saying that."

His eyes flashed, the niceties were over and his rage was boiling. "I'm gonna kick your ass, gringo," he said as he started out the door.

The .45 all but jumped into my hand and I aimed it at his expansive belly. "I would be willing to see if you could follow through with that threat, but we are a little outnumbered here, maybe another time."

He stopped but a big smile slipped across his face. "That thing ain't gonna help you a bit against fifty riders."

I smiled back. "Oh, it will help because if anyone makes a move toward us I am putting the first two rounds in that fat gut of yours. If I were to get hit by something, I will still get two rounds in you." I heard a distant rumble. "Besides, I think you have a bigger problem," I said as I raised my hand for the twenty-five riders to come down.

They started down the hill and I heard Kenny and his group coming in. Soon over a hundred bikers filled the parking lot, and stepping off their bikes they started toward us. Kenny broke off a group of them and sent them around to the other door. I think Julio almost pissed himself; his whole club was trapped inside the bar. Julio was caught completely off guard and started to go inside the bar until I stopped him.

"Okay, enough of this macho crap. We are here for one thing and one thing only: send Casper out. We will take him and leave you to your afternoon tea," I said with a poor Brit accent.

"He isn't here; I haven't seen him since yesterday," he said shakily.

I believed him but I couldn't let it go with that.

"Okay, five of my riders are going inside and check. Have all your riders come out of the bar and stand over next to the porch."

He looked at me wishing he were close enough to gut me then said something to his big friend. "You got trouble coming…from me," he said.

I told Kenny to take four other riders and go through the bar then had Snake take a couple of riders and check out the bikers as they came out of the bar. "So, where is the traitor?" I asked.

Julio stood quietly for a minute. "What the hell, he isn't my problem. He took the cash we paid him and went across the border. Try one of the bars in Boy's Town. TJ, this is your last freebie; next time we meet you and I are going to settle our little differences."

"We certainly will. Where do you want the remains sent?" I looked around to the riders then to Kenny. "Send most of the riders back to wait for us then round up about ten and let's go to Mexico."

I turned back to Julio. "Right now I will call us even but if you hide Casper, I will consider it a debt you won't want to pay. I promise you this, from now on, anyone who hides Casper will get the same thing he does," I said as I looked at the big Mexican.

"TJ, you have shown me great disrespect in front of my men. I don't know that I can call that even," he replied as he looked at me.

I looked around. "I have over a hundred riders. I think it was very wise of you to open your doors to us. You kept your men from being hurt or killed. You prevented a war that would end by people being hurt. After this is all over, we will get together on neutral ground; if you want to get it on then, we do it," I said as I held out my hand.

He looked at it and just before I was going to withdraw it, he took it. "I will go with that. You and I settle this between just the two of us. That is the way it should be anyway; our men should not fight our fights."

"Okay, my men are heading out. You aren't going to interfere in any way? It would be very bad if Jimmy had to send his brothers in blue here to take care of this place," I said.

Just then the CB in the truck squawked; it was Jimmy. I jumped in the truck. "I missed that, Jimmy, come back," I said into the mic.

"One of the border guards said he went across the border about three hours ago," he said.

"Okay, Jimmy, meet us at the border. We have an idea where he is," I told him. He said he would wait on the other side.

Kenny came up next to the truck. "I have ten riders plus me. Let's go," he said and took off before I could respond.

As usual the border cops looked the bikers over pretty closely. I guess they feared ten bikers would try to take over Mexico. Jimmy was just on the other side of the border waiting for us and joined the group. We cruised over to Boy's Town and down the main area of bars. We didn't see Casper's bike, but I did see the kid who had watched our bikes so when we got up near him I got out of the truck and walked over to him. I pulled a twenty from my wallet and waved it in front of him. "Have you seen a white chopper around here today?" I asked.

He looked at the twenty. "Yes," he replied and made a grab for the twenty.

"Come on, you don't get it that easy. Where is he now?" I asked.

"Why are you looking for him?" the young boy asked.

"He did something very wrong to someone in the club and we have to talk to him. If you know where he is, it would only be right to tell us. We will find him sooner or later, so you might as well get the twenty," I told him.

He looked thoughtfully at me and then the other riders. "He was at the ABC earlier but he left with Louisa, I think to her house." This time when he went for the twenty I let it go.

I pulled another twenty from my wallet. "Where does Louisa live?"

"You promise you won't hurt her? She is just trying to make money too."

"We are only after him; we don't want to hurt anyone who doesn't want to hurt us," I told him. He told us where she lived and how best to get there without being seen so I gave him the twenty and we headed for Louisa's house, right there in Boy's Town.

It's hard to sneak up on someone with ten choppers rumbling down the street so I wasn't surprised to see Casper run from Louisa's house when we were a block away. He straddled the bike, fired it up and took off. The other bikers, led by Kenny and Jimmy, sped past the van and gave chase. Casper had a pretty small lead on the pack, but his bike was quick and he was deciding the route so he slowly extended his lead.

I was certain he would turn back toward the border, and I decided to take a different route to try to beat him back there. I told Snake where to turn and guided him back toward the border. Casper, however, didn't do what I expected, and I was soon left far behind by the pack. Damn, I missed my bike now.

Now I was forced to go through town, putting me even further behind. Jimmy squawked back to let us know they were heading out of town. I answered him and told him and Kenny to do nothing to him before I got there, if they caught him.

We finally got through town and Snake dropped the hammer on the old van. It hit a hundred and began shaking so bad he had to back off a bit but kept it going as fast as he dared. Jimmy called back to let us know they had turned onto a dirt side road and then faded. I knew they were quite a distance behind them now and was lucky to see the bike tracks leading off the main road.

After almost an hour, we finally caught up to them. Casper was laying face down on the ground, five riders standing around him.

When we stopped I got out of the truck afraid they had already dealt with him; then I saw him move.

I walked over and kicked him hard in the shoulder to turn him over. "Hello, Casper, did you have a nice ride?"

"You leave me alone, man. You don't have any right to do this. I'm not even a member of your stupid-assed club," he whined. "You mess with me, and the Dark Soldiers will be on you."

I reached down and pulled his colors from his back, the patch looked like it was made by a kid with crayons. "Do you mean Julio and his kiddy club? He had the honor of meeting the entire club today. Who do you think gave you up? He was very helpful. By the way, there are over a hundred bikers waiting for you on the other side of the border." I turned and threw the colors into the van. "Besides, you know you can't just walk away from the club without permission—that will be another charge against you."

"You can't do this. I am in Mexico. It would be kidnapping if you took me across the border," he said near tears.

"You're right, it is kidnapping and if you ever have the opportunity to talk to a cop, you be sure and tell them all about it," I told him.

He tried to get up and was rewarded with a boot to the kidneys. I told Kenny to get him tied up and gagged then throw him into the van. I would ride his bike back. In short order they had him trussed up like a pig ready for market and literally threw him into the van.

"Okay, we ride behind the van just in case he tries anything. We will meet the rest of the club on the other side and ride for home. Jimmy, now would be a good time for you to go home—having you around for this won't help your career," I told him.

He took off the colors and handed them to me. "Thanks. I will go ahead of you and clear the path at the border. From there on, I know nothing about you guys."

"Jimmy, you are welcome at the club any time and if you ever want a set of these back all you have to do is ask," I said holding up the colors. I stood there for a minute waiting for Jimmy to get out of sight then turned to the riders. "Nothing happens before we get back to the clubhouse. He is still a member and deserves the right to defend his actions. Let's go."

I grabbed Casper's helmet and pulled his bike from the ground. Hitting the dirt had done little more than scratch it a bit so I dusted off the seat and fired it up. It felt good to be back in the saddle again, even if it wasn't my own. We rolled back through town and to the border; Jimmy was standing with some of the border cops, and we were waved through without a question. I waved at Jimmy then saw the other bikers waiting for us. I rode the lead as we headed back to Corpus.

The wind hitting me felt good; it was almost like blowing all the tension and stress from my body. As I rode I began considering what was going to happen to Casper. I knew what I wanted to do; I wanted to kill him slowly, very slowly, but I had a problem. According to my agreement I was part of the legal force until this thing was over and with that I couldn't do or be a part of what I wanted. Jean Marie was right in the middle. I knew she understood how I felt but she had a job to do and I didn't want to hurt her. This was going to be a tough one.

I wished I had a camera when we rolled through Freer. The cop was sitting in front of the courthouse and was completely freaked by having a hundred bikers rolling through his town; I almost fell off the bike laughing. Just after we passed through Freer, Jimmy pulled in front of us and rolled out ahead for home.

It was dark by the time we got to the clubhouse, and I was surprised to see Jean Marie there in the parking lot. She walked over to me not even noticing the bike not being the one I usually ride. "Where's Casper?" she asked.

I stepped purposely away from the bike. "We went to Laredo to find him but we discovered he had gone across the border into Mexico."

She guided me away from the others. "TJ, you realize you are officially a part of law enforcement. You can't go down there and bring him back."

"I am fully aware of that. If I did that, any arrest

would be thrown out. You know, you seem to think I am just some brain-dead biker. Believe it or not I do have a bit of a brain," I told her.

She looked at me, a question on her face but it never reached her lips. "No, I never said that. TJ, I am afraid for you; I understand your allegiance to the club, really I do, but if you cross the line on this thing with Casper, you are breaking the law you swore to uphold."

"What you know about me could be put in a thimble and still have room for your finger. You don't know a damned thing about who I am. Nothing. And yet you think you know what I am going to do."

"I know enough to recognize you have some issues here. Just think before you do something, TJ. Don't screw up your life. Would Roger have wanted that?"

"Don't talk to me about Roger. You were the one who talked me into involving him in this; you are the one who didn't think I should go this alone. If you had left me alone Roger would still be alive and I wouldn't need to chase Casper down for this. So just stay off my case." I was near screaming.

"Thanks, TJ, I needed a reminder of what happened to Roger, but I don't want the same thing to happen to you. Just forget about Casper until he gets back on this side. Then let us take care of it," she said.

I looked at her, forcing myself not to smile. "I promise I will not go down to Mexico to get Casper."

"And you won't send your people after him?" she asked.

"My word on it," I answered.

She looked at me sideways. "You're hiding something but I don't have time to mess with it. I am sending word to Laredo to have them watch for Casper. If you hear anything from him or about him I expect to hear from you."

"You just do your job. I'll be right here," I told her as she walked away.

We waited until she was gone for a few minutes. "Okay, get Casper inside."

Snake and two of the riders went to the van, but it was Snake who dragged him out of the van and into the clubhouse. "What do I do with him, TJ?"

I looked around the room. "Tie him to that chair and put the chair on the table," I told him then looked around the room. "This is club business. For those of you who rode with us today I thank you and any time you want to ride with the club you are welcome, but this is something that can't be witnessed by an outsider."

A few of the riders grumbled but they started toward the door. One of the riders stopped and came over to me. "TJ, my name is Danny. Thank you for allowing us to be a part of this. I will be back, I want to ride with you guys as a member."

I reached out a hand. "Danny, you are welcome to ride with us; prove yourself and there is a place for you as a member." He shook my hand then headed for the door.

I walked over to the table where Casper had been placed. "Okay, let's quiet down. If you want a beer or a drink get it now and someone bring me one." Most of the riders headed for the beer locker. "In a few minutes we will take care of business. Someone get Casper some water."

When things quieted down I took a long hit on my beer and stood on a chair. The room got deadly quiet. I looked around the room. "Okay, the first thing we need to clear up are the charges against Casper. Number one is using the club name and facilities for personal profit, specifically for making methamphetamines. This charge is reason for expulsion from the club and a fine equal to seventy-five percent of the profits he made. Second is abandoning the club without addressing this intent with the club. For this he will have to walk the gauntlet if found guilty as well as forfeiture of his motorcycle to the club. The third charge is murdering a friend of mine, knowing he was a friend. Since this does not really fall under our written guidelines the punishment is to be determined by this gathering. Last he is charged with murdering Eddie, president of this club. If found guilty, his life is yours to do with as you please."

The entire gathering began yelling for his life. It took a good ten minutes to get them under control again. I held up my hands. "Before the hearing there is one more bit of business to take care of. When Eddie died I took over the club because I was the last remaining original member and my intent was to stay in that position only temporarily. The club guidelines allow a standing president to name his successor. With that in mind I am naming Kenny as president of CC Riders to take over right now." I motioned for Kenny to come up.

"I can't explain why, at least not right now," I continued, "but I have to leave this gathering. No one is to inform me as to any action that is taken by the club where this is concerned. Allow me to say one thing before I go. Be careful with what you decide and how you carry it out," I said as I stepped down to Kenny. "Kenny, I'm taking Casper's bike to the house. Someone can pick it up there. Call me when whatever punishment has been decided but don't tell me the decision; you know why."

"I got ya, bro. I will talk to you later," he said as he shook my hand and I left the clubhouse.

I went out the door and grabbed Casper's bike then turned it toward the house. I walked into the apartment leaving the lights off, went over to the bar and found the scotch. I poured a rocks glass full then held it up in toast. "Here's to you, Roger, friend for far too short a time and yet a friend for life." I drank down the glass then poured another. "To you, Eddie, brothers not by blood but by choice," then downed that glass.

I poured another glass and lay back in my chair and slowly drifted off. For the first time in weeks I slept for seven hours straight, but when I started to stand up my legs felt like they were both asleep. I went back to the bathroom and allowed the water to heat up in the shower then climbed in and allowed the heat to take the stiffness from my body.

For the next two days I just enjoyed riding and working at the Blue Note. It felt like life was slowly returning to normal. In the evening of the second day I was sitting in the Blue Note when Kenny came in and sat down. "It's over, bro. Are you sure you don't want to know?"

"Nope, the end is the end," I said. "For me it is over."

CHAPTER EIGHTEEN

I called Jean Marie and arranged to meet with her at the Blue Note. When she came in I was nursing my third beer. She sat across from me, and I started right in. "Jean Marie, I said some pretty terrible things to you the last time we talked. I'm sorry."

She ordered coffee. "Yes, you did, but I do understand. We were taking advantage of your relationship with the club and putting you in a very precarious position, but believe it or not we have always been there for you."

"Well, you don't have to be there any longer; it's over. The meth lab is closed down and you have two of the three in custody," I explained.

She smiled. "Yes, we do, and they have laid out the whole thing for us and pleaded guilty to both the manufacture and distribution of methamphetamines. They both also pointed to Casper for both Eddie and Roger, but we don't have Casper."

"I have a feeling you can pretty much scratch Casper. He made a big sale before he went to Mexico; he could live a very long time down there on that," I told her.

"So, your job is over?" she asked.

"That's the way I see it. I need for you to make arrangements for the meeting, away from the base and away from the cop shop," I requested.

She looked me directly in the eye, "Are you

absolutely certain you don't know where Casper is, or what has happened to him?"

"I can absolutely guarantee I don't have the slightest idea where Casper is or anything about what he is doing now," I told her honestly.

"TJ, what has changed? Just a few days ago you had blood in your eyes for Casper, now you just walk away from it? I don't buy it."

"Don't get me wrong, Jean Marie. If I ever see Casper I will be happy to arrange a meeting between him and Saint Peter but I am not going to waste any more time on him."

She took a drink of her coffee and made a face like she wanted to spit it back into the cup. "I know better than to drink this crap. I get the feeling you aren't being completely straight with me but I don't have any proof so, yes, I will make the arrangements."

That night I hit the wind and decided to just do some cruising. The freedom of the ride was exhilarating and allowed me to clear my head over what had happened over the last year. As the old stuff was blowing away a thought hit me: Sandy! I almost dumped the bike spinning it around and heading for the apartment. I couldn't get there fast enough.

I called Jimmy to get Sandy's telephone number and dialed her number. I almost choked when she answered. I cleared my throat. "Sandy? This is TJ."

She was silent for so long I thought she had hung up. When she did answer her voice was a little shaky as though she wasn't sure she wanted to talk to me. "Hi TJ. How did you get my number? I don't remember giving it to you."

I hadn't thought about this. "I, uh…well, a uh…friend kinda gave it to me."

"A friend? A friend of mine or a friend of yours? Oh, wait, you don't know any of my friends, so it must be one of your friends, but none of your friends know me. So, would you like to try again? Who gave you my number?"

Was she going to be upset at Jimmy for giving me her number? I guess I really had no choice. "We have one mutual friend," I told her.

She was quiet for a minute. "No, you have a friend and I have a brother. Is that who gave you my number without asking me?" she asked.

"I uh...I mean...well, yes, I asked Jimmy for it," I told her.

There was silence on the other end then she started laughing. "Big bad TJ, stuttering like a school boy asking for a first date. It's okay. I told Jimmy I would like to talk to you. So, has the big mystery ended?"

"Thanks, I just didn't want to get Jimmy into trouble. Yeah, it is pretty much over, but I still can't really tell you much."

"Still don't trust me? Okay, I'll accept that for now but don't expect me to drop it."

"Okay, I can live with that. Hey, I would really like to sit down and talk sometime. Would you be open to that?" I asked.

"Well, I was thinking about making a run out to Mustang Island tomorrow evening. It would be nice to have someone there just in case I get stuck in the sand," she answered.

I smiled remembering the night we met. "I will be there. I would hate to have you get out there and not be able to make it back." We talked for a few minutes more then rang off.

It felt good to have a normal conversation with someone and just be myself; for over a year I had lived in a very dark place. It seemed that no matter what I did, I was always having to hide who I was even from people I had been very close to at one time.

The telephone broke my concentration. "Hello?"

"TJ, this is Sherry. I just got a call from Roger's lawyer. He wants to meet with us as soon as possible."

"Well, I talked to Jean Marie earlier to set up a meeting with the Navy and the government. I can't do anything before I hear from her," I told her.

"She called me earlier. You are meeting here at the bar at one tomorrow afternoon. Can we meet with the lawyers tomorrow, here, say nine in the morning?" she asked.

I thought about it; I still hadn't decided what I was going to do about the Navy. My enlistment had expired while I was on this assignment and I still didn't know what I was going to do. "Okay, I guess tomorrow morning is fine. I'll get all this over in a day and I can decide what I'm going to do with the rest of my life."

There was a moment's silence. "So, TJ, what do *you* want to do?"

"I don't know. I guess I'll stick with the Navy. It's a job."

"No, I mean what do you really want to do? Regardless of job or anything else, what would you do?" she asked.

I didn't even have to think about the answer. "I would ride until the wheels fell off my bike or my ass hurt so much I couldn't stand it."

"Well, then do what you want to do. I will see you tomorrow morning," she said then hung up.

I really wanted to talk to Sandy again but it was getting late so I decided just to call it a night and crash. The heat of the shower relaxed me more than I would have imagined and sleep came to me rather quickly.

The next morning I slept until almost eight then rushed over to the bar. Sherry's car was the only one in the lot so I parked next to her and went inside. I went into the office and poured myself a cup of coffee, took a sip and spit it back into the cup. "How in the hell can anyone make coffee that tastes this damned bad?" I asked.

She laughed. "I thought you Navy guys could handle bad coffee."

"Bad, yeah, but this stuff is beyond bad. If the world ever runs out of paint stripper you will never have to work again," I said. Just then the bell at the front door went off.

Sherry got up and walked out of the office returning with two well-dressed men behind her, undoubtedly lawyers from the looks of the thousand-dollar suits and Italian loafers. One of the men held out his right hand. As we shook hands he handed me a business card. "My name is Robert Harris and this is my brother and partner Richard."

Introductions were made all around and Sherry offered them chairs. I was impressed by these two; they were in a bar that was obviously well below their standard and yet it was obvious neither of them was the least bit uncomfortable. Robert opened his briefcase then asked each of us for identification. "I wouldn't normally have to ask but we don't know either of you."

I smiled. "No problem. Now, what is this all about?" I asked. "I mean I know Roger named us in his will but I didn't really think much about it."

Robert smiled and looked at Richard then back at us. "Mr. Hamlin, Ms. Davis, allow me to explain. Mr. Morris's wife died a number of years ago and they never had any children. Mr. Morris was an only child and up until a few months ago all of his holdings were going to a few dozen different charities. He came into our office and changed his will, indicating all of his property and holdings are to be transferred to you. In fact he transferred his house in Corpus and that property to you at that time along with everything in the house, the cars, the apartment you are living in. The two of you are to share equally in all that he has."

My heart was thumping in my chest. I looked at Sherry not knowing what to say and just tilted my chair onto its back legs.

She finally asked, "How…how much are you talking about?"

"Well, stocks, bonds, cash and insurance comes to about seventeen million," he said as though he was telling the time of day. My chair went out from under me and I slammed against the floor along with it. Both men jumped up and helped me to my feet. "Are you okay, sir?"

The rest of the meeting went by without me really hearing anything else; I signed papers I didn't read as Sherry instructed me and we were given a list of all Roger's assets, locations of other property he owned along with deeds and where to find keys, maps and such.

"There was one particular request Roger had for you two. The house, as we said, belongs to you, Mr. Hamlin, but all of the other property is to be held jointly by the two of you for at least ten years."

I was completely lost; I couldn't even form

words. Richard Harris handed me an envelope. "This contains keys to the house and the location and combinations for the safes."

I took the envelope and finally was able to say, "Thank you."

The two men left and I walked back into Sherry's office, found her bottle and filled my coffee cup. I knocked down about half of the amber liquid then turned to Sherry. "Did I really hear those numbers right?"

She wrapped her arms around me and pulled me close. "You heard right, TJ, you heard right. I knew Roger was special, never knew just how special. So, what are you going to do now?"

"I am going to take a very long ride then come back here tonight and ask you if this is all true," I told her.

"You better make that a short ride, you have a meeting here in just over an hour," she told me.

"Damn, forgot about that," I said then started laughing.

She looked at me like I was crazy. "What is so funny?"

"Last night you asked me what I would do if...and here we are; money is no longer a part of the equation." I began laughing again.

"So, what are you going to do?"

"Enjoy the hell out of this meeting. I can't wait," I said as I finished my drink and poured another.

"Well, you better get something to eat before the meeting or you are going to be a mess. I'll drive," she said taking my drink and leading the way out the door.

I ate slowly, intentionally making it back to the bar fifteen minutes late. Two government representatives, Jean Marie, Captain Joseph and a Naval Admiral were waiting in the parking lot when we arrived. "Hey! The gang's all here. Come in, I'm buying for everyone! It's a day of celebration," I said.

As we sat around a table the captain and admiral asked if Sherry had some coffee. She started to say something, but I jumped in. "Sure, I think there is a fresh pot in the office." Sherry first frowned at me then smiled, as did Jean Marie.

"Coffee sounds good," said the two government agents. It took all I had to keep from laughing. Everyone else opted for something cold and I went back to the office for the bottle.

One of the government agents was the first to speak. "Mr. Hamlin, the United States Government thanks you for putting these people out of business. Perhaps a little nonconventional, but it seems to have had the desired result, except for Mr. Carr, of course."

"I am sure he will screw up in the future and someone will nail him," I said.

Captain Joseph took a drink of his coffee, almost choked on it but made a quick recovery. "Petty Officer Hamlin, as soon as you get a haircut and report back to the base, we will advance you of course, and you have a few special awards coming. We look forward to having you back. Your service will, of course, be unbroken."

I knocked down my drink and poured another then held up my cup in salute. "To the Corpus Christi Police Department, it has been a pleasure. I have learned a lot from the last year and I am thankful it is over." I took a drink. I turned to the government guys. "You guys got what you wanted: a resolution. Thank you for all your wonderful support." I took another drink. Then I turned to Joseph. "Sir, with all due respect, the Navy can kiss my ass. All you could worry about was my haircut. Well, I have been out of your Navy for over six months and I will not be returning; just send my discharge papers." I took another drink, set my cup down and walked out of the bar.

I stepped across my true love, fired her up and hit the wind.

EPILOGUE

I did meet Sandy on Mustang Island that night. We sat on the beach listening to the waves crash on the beach. I never noticed before how different it sounds when you can't see the waves break. I explained to her that I was going to be gone for a while, that I was taking the next few months to just cruise. I had been in the Navy for four years and I just needed time for me and spend some time thinking about what I wanted to do with the rest of my life, at least for the foreseeable future. We agreed that we would touch base when I returned, though I made certain she was aware I didn't know when that would be.

I spent the next few months just blowing around with no particular place to go. Hey, didn't Chuck Berry write a song by that name back in 1964? Anyway, it was a good time for me; it almost seemed like each mile blew all my problems away. I won't go into details about the trip, not yet, but I did meet some wonderful, and some not so wonderful, people on my short adventure.

When I walked into the Blue Note months later, Sherry showed me an article from the local newspaper about a body being found back in the dunes on Padre Island. They couldn't identify the body but the person had been dressed in jeans held up by a "Live to Ride, Ride to Live" belt buckle. The report said the cause of death couldn't be determined, but evidence indicated the man had been buried alive in the hot sand dune. Ouch!

I ended up buying Eddie's bike shop. I didn't figure I would make much from it, but I was able to put some of the guys back to work and hired a couple of other club members to work there. Not knowing whether I would have the time and not really having a great business sense, I hired Kenny and Snake to run the place. Who knows, maybe there will be a future in custom bikes.

Shauna committed herself to long-term rehab and will be returning home next month. She and Kenny are even talking about making their relationship permanent. I told Kenny I would rent the Blue Note for them and cover any costs. Sherry said we would share that cost.

Dave is doing well, and I did make it out to see the family, so my private parts are safe for the time being. Dave received a check from an unknown source that allowed him to make some much needed repairs to the bait shop and move him and his family to their own home.

I called Jean Marie and apologized for leaving without really thanking her, but she seemed to understand and promised she would see me at the bar one day.

Sherry and I became partners in the Blue Note. We were going to improve it but decided to buy some property on Padre Island Drive just a few hundred yards from Dave's. Maybe we will build a larger club with a dining room.

Oh, and I found both of Roger's safes, I didn't even bother counting the cash that was there, but I would say most people could have lived comfortably on that alone. I now live in the main house. It took me a long time to bring myself to move in; even now I still feel as though it is Roger's and I am an intruder. I keep expecting him to walk in and tell me I need to leave, though I doubt he would have ever done that anyway.

I got better with my music. I had plenty of time and spent many hours practicing. I was enjoying the new life, a life so close to carefree that it was almost sinful. I rode when I felt like riding, drank when I felt like drinking, and lived a life few could even dream of.

Yes sir, I was living the life of Riley. Little did any of us know that a storm was coming that would blow it all away.

Read a Preview of Riding Into the Storm, Book Two in The TJ Series

Chapter 1

Six months on the road is a great way to wash away pain, as long as you are smart about it. Unfortunately, I wasn't always smart with my time away. That was my plan, to take six months and just be a bum. The morning I left Corpus I had no real destination in mind and really didn't much care where I ended up. This brings to mind something the owner of a gas station where I had worked said when he was reminding me of my lack of focus on my life: "A man who has no destination will never know when he has arrived." That little tidbit of truth never entered my mind when I fired up my Harley and said goodbye to any responsibility for the time being.

As I said, I had no plan so I just headed west, mostly because I didn't really know anyone in that direction, and I eventually found myself in El Paso. I don't remember being there before this trip but it seemed so familiar. The first night there I found a bar that suited me quite well, since liquor by the drink was only allowed in private clubs. This bar, for a few dollars, allowed customers to bring their own bottle into the bar. This is a pretty common business; some just charge boosted prices for the mixers. It was only a few yards from a liquor store so it became my hangout for a few days

The first night I was there, a young dancer sat down at my table and asked if she could have a drink; I paid a jacked up price for her mixer and we started talking. I knew I was being foolish. I was certain an attractive gal like her had a boyfriend, but I ignored my own intelligence and started spending every night there with her. When one of the men sitting at the stage watching the dancers made a grab for her while she was dancing, I flew to the stage and put the man on the ground quickly. Understandably, I was asked to leave the premises and not return.

I was about ready to leave El Paso when I stopped in at a bar that advertised a live band, so I grabbed a bottle of single malt and settled in. The first night the band was pretty good but the lead guitarist lacked some very basic transitional skills. As the band was breaking down, I went over to talk to him. At first I he blew me off as a know-it-all, but when I asked to see his guitar and showed him what I was talking about, he began paying attention. He introduced himself as James and we headed out to a Night Owl's Club for a few drinks. While we were there he asked if I would meet with the band and go through a few numbers.

The next afternoon I spent two hours having more fun than I had in a long time as we joined together and had a great jam session. James was a pretty good guitarist and we spent a lot of time playing together, but I noticed the bass sound was a bland thump, thump, thump. I picked up the bass and started playing what felt good with the music and soon they picked up on the sound and that night came together and blew the place away. I stayed around and even played with the band a few times over the next few weeks but the itch got to me and I blew town again.

Once again on the road, I started heading northeast and eventually found myself on the road to

Amarillo. About twenty-five miles from town, I passed a half dozen bikes at a way stop. As I passed I saw the riders going for their bikes. That was when I realized I had on my CC Riders patch. I reached back and found one of the little 380s in the backpack strapped to my sissy bar and slipped it into my inside jacket pocket. I looked in my mirror and saw them coming up fast. I was certain I could out run them without any trouble but decided to just cruise through it and see what happened.

The riders flowed around me but I didn't feel any fear, they weren't acting in an aggressive manner. About fifteen miles later the lead rider raised his arm and pointed toward a building ahead on the right side of the road. The riders broke into single file and the lead rider motioned for me to join them so I dropped in behind the last bike. That was really the first time I noticed they wore no patch. When I pulled up, the lead biker walked over and held out his hand. "I'm Jerry," he said. I took his hand and introduced myself.

As we strolled into the bar I was introduced to Mike, Stephen, Carl and David. After admiring each other's rides we went in and grabbed a couple of tables on the back wall, and I allowed my new friends to buy me a Lone Star. Jerry sat next to me, "Where are you from, TJ?"

I took a long hit on the cold brew and allowed it to wash the dust from my throat, "Corpus Christi is home but I have lived all over South Texas."

"So, what brings you all the way to Amarillo, exploring the Northern regions?"

I shook my head, "No, I just needed to get on the road for a while and blow off some bad dust. I got out of the Navy a few months ago and went back to my home town but going home just isn't possible."

"I know what you mean. I left the Marine Corps a little over a year ago and just recently settled down. You spent some time in country, patrol boats or aviation?"

"I spent fourteen months on river patrol riding as fore gunner," I explained.

He nodded toward the other riders. "Most of the guys who ride with us are vets. Who are the CC Riders?"

"Some of us formed a club before I joined the Navy. It started out as just a dozen or so riders, but we have close to a hundred riders now."

"Is it a 1% club?"

I shook my head. "No. Don't get me wrong. They are true brothers but don't go for the outlaw stuff. Other clubs around the area know us and that we aren't into their business and not interested in conflict. They also know if they come at us, we aren't the only ones to get hurt."

He laughed. "I don't imagine so but you are out here solo right now, so I would strongly suggest you bag your patch. We do have a club or two around here who would love to rip it."

I thought about that for a minute. I had been rather foolish. "You're right. I'm so used to riding around home I didn't think about it." I removed my leather jacket and pulled the cutoff from it and folded it inside out. I took the little 380 and slipped it into my right hip pocket.

For the next couple of hours we drank, played pool and told tall tales, just having a good time. It was just about dusk when we heard the other motorcycles roll into the parking lot. I looked at Jerry. "Some of your riders?"

He shook his head. "I don't think so. Come on,

let's get out of here."

When you are in another man's town the smart thing to do is follow his lead so I grabbed my jacket and folded up colors and followed him toward the door. Three bikers about the size of the Rocky Mountains came through the door as we approached.

The three men stopped and looked around the room. One of them looked in our direction. "Who belongs to those bikes out there?"

Before I could stop myself I snapped at him, "Well, let's see there, Einstein, there are ten customers in this bar and since they don't belong to you they must be ours."

I knew I had just screwed up but this was no time to back down. He walked so close to me I could smell the stench of sweat rolling from his body. He pushed me back, separating me from the others. "Well, Slick, you seem to be the big man around town. You ready to take a beating for being such a wise ass? I hope so because my bike's acting up and I'm looking for something else to hang my tag on."

He had me at close quarters. I couldn't get any leverage to throw any kind of effective punch. I eased my hand back and hooked my thumb in my rear pocket. He could see the knife on my belt, and I was certain he expected me to go for it. Instead I wrapped my fingers around the butt of the little Walther and pulled it from my pocket levering back the hammer as I shoved the barrel under his chin. "I'm sorry there cowgirl. I like my ride and if you ever sat on her she would puke all over you."

His friends were none too happy and started reaching for something. "Don't do it. I have absolutely no problem bouncing a hollow point around inside his skull," I said, and they eased off.

I looked at Jerry. "You guys get on down the road. I'll blow out of here when I can't hear your bikes any more. Thanks for the beer. Maybe you guys will get to the beach one day." I reached inside my pocket and tossed Jerry the keys. "Fire mine up if you will. I think I'll be leaving in a hurry."

The two other men finally stepped back. It was a couple of minutes before I heard the bikes come to life and they began rolling on down the highway. I pushed a little harder into the man's chin. "I'm getting out of here. If someone comes through that door before I get on the road, they're going to get stung. Oh, and if I see you coming after me, there is a larger barrel just waiting to be fired up."

When I got to the door I kicked the man as hard as I could and ran toward my bike. Jerry was right there next to my bike ready to go. "You don't have to hurry man," then he looked back at the three other motorcycles. All three rear wheels were chained together, the chain locked with a substantial looking padlock. I threw the big bike in gear and twisted the grip hard sending back a rooster tail of dirt and pebbles. I was back in my habitat, the open road.

We ran for a few more miles then cruised through part of Amarillo stopping at a bar where twenty or so bikes filled the parking lot. I looked at Jerry. "I hope these are your friends and not theirs."

He laughed as he dropped his helmet on his sissy bar. "No sweat, man. These are my people."

The bar was loud and filled with the laughter of people having a good time. We grabbed a beer and joined a group of guys gathered around a stage drooling over a sweet Latina chick, who was shaking it like there was no tomorrow. As we stood there he introduced me to some of the guys there. The one named Rayburn stood there next to us for a while then asked me where I was from. I told him and we moved away from the noise of the music and sat at the bar.

"What's your story, man?" Rayburn asked.

I took a long hit on the beer before answering. "No story. I just blew town a month or so ago to get some bad stuff out of my head."

"I know that feeling. Problem is I can't afford to just jump and go." Then he told me his story; he had been a tunnel rat in country and ended up being discharged on a medical after a booby trap took out the man in front of him, scattering parts and mess all over him. It was more than a few minutes before he noticed some of the blood was his own. He spent some time in vets and was sent home with a Purple Heart and a thank you from Uncle Sam. Since he returned, he had not been able to keep a job and just recently finished a stretch of counseling for post-traumatic stress syndrome. Now that he feels better there are no jobs for him.

We had been talking for over an hour when I looked up at a television sitting behind the bar. On the screen a weatherman pointed out a storm that was rolling over Cuba. I got the bartender's attention. "Can you turn that up please?"

He turned up the television. "They have been talking about that most of the day. It looks like the Gulf Coast could take a serious hit." It was the end of July, a little early in the hurricane season, but that didn't mean they were weak.

I thought about Sherry, the bar, the club and Dave and wondered what they were feeling. I went to the pay phone and dialed the Blue Note. Sherry picked up. "Sherry, what are they saying down there about the storm?"

There was a mumbled sound as she covered the mouthpiece and spoke to someone. "Sorry about that. We really don't know much. The storm is slamming Cuba right now, and they expect it to weaken after that. They say we may get hit with a high category one or low two."

"Okay, I will be there as fast as I can. I am in Amarillo right now."

Her voice became stern. "TJ, we're okay. Stay where you are. There is no sense in you driving into a storm you can't stop. There's nothing you can do here until the storm passes anyway."

"After the storm they may not allow me in, and if phone lines and power go there is no way to get in touch. I would rather be there."

"Quit being an ass. You needed to get away. You still need that down time. Give me a phone number where I can reach you, and I promise I will call as soon as possible after the storm."

I looked at the number on the pay phone and gave it to her. "I'll be here. You better be in touch or I will need more down time after I go nuts." We talked a few more minutes and hung up.

I went back to the bar but I was a basket case, my nerves right on the surface. There was no way could I just sit there. I finished my beer, set down the bottle, and said, "I have to get out of here. All my people are down there."

I walked over to Jerry, thanked him, explained why I had to make a fast run south then headed toward the door. Rayburn caught me before I got there. "If you can cover gas I'll be happy to make the run with you. Just let me stop by my sister's place and grab some gear."

I was in a hurry, but the ride would be better with

a little company. Of course there was the fact I didn't know this man who just admitted to me that he had some issues. "Rayburn, I appreciate that but I am going to be running hard and I don't think you want to tag along on a ride like this. Besides, I can't be marking time while I wait for you."

"I'll keep up. Look, I've been marking time here for months and nothing is coming my way. My sister's place is on the way to the interstate. The stop won't take five minutes. If it's the cash I will see if my sister can spot me a few dollars." He was right on my heels as I moved toward the door.

I am pretty good at figuring people out, and he seemed like a good guy who just might need a break. "What the hell, let's go grab your stuff and get on the road. Don't worry about the cash. I got you. I don't want to say this but I'm going to. Just don't mess me over. If you do it, I will eventually win."

"I have no doubt about that, bro."

True to his word his sister's place was right near the freeway and he was in and out in little over five minutes. We jumped over to a gas station, topped off our tanks and settled in for the seven-hundred mile trip south. As soon as we hit the highway I rolled the throttle up to eighty-five and settled in. Rayburn pulled alongside me and motioned for me to slow down then he took the lead. He had us down to about five miles over the posted speed limit and I wanted to blow past him; if he couldn't keep up I didn't need him tagging along.

A Mustang pulled around and blew past us and once again I wanted to roll the throttle so I pulled up beside Rayburn, but once again he motioned for me to slow down. A few miles up the road I saw flashing red lights on top of an Oldsmobile and in front of that car was the Mustang that dusted us. A half mile up the road he opened up and we were back to eighty-five again. I mentally thanked the gods that watch over fools and allowed Rayburn to lead the way.

When we made a gas stop I realized I hadn't eaten in a while and seriously doubted my road partner had either. There were a few eighteen-wheelers in the lot so we decided to give the greasy spoon a chance for a quick meal. When we walked in all eyes turned to us. I felt like a bug in a glass and wanted to ask them what the hell they were looking at but I didn't have time for confrontation.

I looked at the menu, a black chalkboard with the day's specials listed. One of the truckers walked over. "Where you boys headed?"

I didn't want to waste time with this fool but again the gods who watch over fools told me to shut up and just answer the question. "On our way to Corpus."

He shook his head, "You know there is a storm brewing and headed toward the gulf. It's already torn the hell out of Cuba."

"That's why we're headed home."

He nodded. "I understand. Okay, take a little advice. Go for the stew, at least it won't have you pulling off to empty your gut in a couple of hours. Here's another piece of advice. About eighteen miles down the road there is a speed trap and another a few miles past that. Watch trucks' headlights; they will tell you if something is close by."

For the first time I really looked at my new best friend; he was tall, six-foot-four or better, weighed in close to three hundred pounds and looked like he could bend a jack handle with his bare hands. Then I looked at his face. Though covered with a full beard that ended about half way to his belt buckle, the amazing part was his eyes. They were filled with smiles and the brightest green I have ever seen on any man. I introduced myself and Rayburn before he went back to his meal. He said his name was Cliff Mason and he hoped our trip was a safe one.

We ordered the stew and sat there and ate like starving men. It wasn't the best I have ever had but it was okay. Before we finished our meal Cliff walked up and put one of his big hands on each of our backs. "I'll be prayin' for you boys. Drive safe."

I turned to him. "I don't hold much with praying. I been down the religious road, can't say I believe anybody is listening."

He never stopped smiling. "That's okay. He knows you, TJ, and I can believe strong enough for us both," then he walked out the door.

Look for The TJ Series Book Two: Riding Into the Storm at your favorite retailer coming soon.

J.R. Hamilton grew up in Corpus Christi, Texas, and lived there until he left school to join the Navy in 1964. After a time in Viet Nam, he was assigned to NAS (Naval Air Station) Corpus Christi and was stationed there for three years. While stationed in Corpus, he managed to get into a little trouble and much of it was due to biking.

He started working on motorcycles when he was 13, an old Triumph 650. He got his hands on a 1959 Panhead and began rebuilding his second motorcycle; this one became the love of his life.

J.R. He has ridden with clubs in Texas, Virginia, Tennessee, Ohio, Maryland, Arkansas, Louisiana, Mississippi, Florida, California, North Carolina, South Carolina, Georgia, and South Dakota, and rode in Daytona's Run for the Sun and the Sturgis Motorcycle Rally in the Black Hills of South Dakota.

facebook.com/jrhamiltonbooks
www.jrhamiltonbooks.com
www.deadkeypublishing.com/jr-hamilton.html